PRAISE FOR
THE GREAT TROUBLE

A *School Library Journal* Best Book of the Year
A CCBC Choice
An NCSS-CBC Notable Social Studies Trade Book for Young People
A Capitol Choices Noteworthy Book for Children and Teens
A Junior Library Guild Selection
Winner of the Oregon Spirit Book Award

★ "Hopkinson illuminates a pivotal chapter in the history of public health. . . . Eel tells his story in a matter-of-fact and accessible manner, making [it] palatable and entertaining."
School Library Journal, Starred

"Plenty of best-of-times goodness shines from the murk. A solid, somber dramatization of a real-life medical mystery."
—*Kirkus Reviews*

"A historical novel of true Dickensian fashion, with vivid descriptions of Victorian London's filthy Thames, foul air, and sickly-looking skies. . . . And like a good Dickensian tale, Eel's story contains twists and turns . . . and an earnest protagonist readers will root for."
—*The Horn Book Magazine*

"A great choice for introducing readers to science and history."
—*Booklist*

"Hopkinson fills her tale with relatable characters, lots of suspense and plenty of details on the everyday life of an orphan living in Victorian London. Best of all, observant readers will notice that they have all the clues they need to find the solution . . . if, like Eel, they know the right questions to ask."
—*BookPage*

ALSO BY DEBORAH HOPKINSON

INTO THE *Firestorm*

A Novel of San Francisco, *1906*

Deborah Hopkinson

THE GREAT TROUBLE

A MYSTERY OF LONDON, the BLUE DEATH, and a BOY CALLED EEL

DEBORAH HOPKINSON

A YEARLING BOOK

In memory of my dear friend Michele Hill,
who, like Dr. John Snow, lived a life dedicated
to truth, compassion, and service

Text copyright © 2013 by Deborah Hopkinson
Cover art copyright © 2013 by Stephanie Dalton Cowan

All rights reserved. Published in the United States by Yearling, an imprint of Random House Children's Books, a division of Random House LLC, a Penguin Random House Company, New York. Originally published in hardcover in the United States by Alfred A. Knopf, an imprint of Random House Children's Books, New York, in 2013.

Yearling and the jumping horse design are registered trademarks of Random House LLC.

Visit us on the Web! randomhousekids.com

Educators and librarians, for a variety of teaching tools,
visit us at RHTeachersLibrarians.com

The Library of Congress has cataloged the hardcover edition of this work as follows:
Hopkinson, Deborah.
The Great Trouble : a mystery of London, the blue death,
and a boy called Eel / Deborah Hopkinson.
p. cm.
Summary: Eel, an orphan, and his best friend Florrie must help Dr. John Snow
prove that cholera is spread through water, and not poisonous air,
when an epidemic sweeps across their London neighborhood in 1854.
ISBN 978-0-375-84818-6 (trade) — ISBN 978-0-375-94818-3 (lib. bdg.) —
ISBN 978-0-449-81819-0 (ebook)
[1. Cholera—Fiction. 2. Epidemics—Fiction. 3. Orphans—Fiction.
4. London (England)—History—19th century—Fiction. 5. Great Britain—
History—Victoria, 1837–1901—Fiction.] I. Title.
PZ7.H778125Gr 2013 [Fic]—dc23 2012032799
ISBN 978-0-375-84308-2 (pbk.)

Printed in the United States of America

10 9 8 7 6

First Yearling Edition 2015

CONTENTS

PART ONE

Mudlark

There is another class who may be termed riverfinders . . . they are commonly known by the name of "mud-larks." . . . They may be seen of all ages . . . crawling among the barges at the various wharfs along the river . . . they are scarcely half covered by the tattered indescribable things that serve them for clothing.

—Henry Mayhew,
London Labour and the London Poor (1851)

CHAPTER ONE
Riverfinders

1854
Monday, August 28

What we now call the Great Trouble began one thick, hot, foul-smelling morning in August. 'Course, I didn't know it then. No one did.

I remember that day for quite another reason.

I was supposed to be dead. But somehow he had found me out.

It was early, and dark enough that most mudlarks weren't on the river yet. I liked this time best. The stink wasn't quite so bad for some reason. And it was quiet, since most folks in London were still sleeping. The bustle and noise of the old city would start up soon enough.

Thumbless Jake was there, of course. The rest of us scavengers wondered if he ever did sleep. And on this particular morning, Jake was on edge, I expect because of spending so much time wading in that sludgy stink we called a river. So when he spied me snatchin' up something shiny from the murky water, he commenced hollering like a mad bull about to charge.

And I should know. I might never have been on a farm in all my nearly thirteen years, but I'd seen my share of raging beasts at the old Smithfield livestock market, a fearful but exciting place. They'd moved it two years before, on account of the mayhem caused by throngs of cattle, pigs, goats, horses, and sheep tramping through the heart of the city. I was sad to see it go.

"Give it here, Eel!" Jake shouted at once. He thrust out his long stick and lunged for my ankles.

"Can't catch me," I taunted. I skittered out of reach, fast as I could, sticky brown mud squelching between my toes. "Don't be greedy. It's just a bit of rope."

"Liar. 'Tain't rope at all. I seen it glitter with me own eyes. That's copper you got there." Thumbless Jake pointed the forefinger of his right hand—his good one—at me. "Play fair, Eel."

"Why should I? No one's ever played fair with me." I said it, but that wasn't quite true. Even Jake himself had once done me a good deed.

"Wicked, ungrateful lad," Jake growled, aiming a huge hunk of spit at me.

4

Jake had been a blacksmith once, or so I'd heard from Ned (we called him Nasty Ned, on account of him being the worst-smelling lad on the river). "Gin was Jake's downfall," Ned had told me. "And then came the day he tippled so much he slammed a great hammer down on 'is own thumb."

I tried to picture Jake's muscles as they must've been, rippling across his back like ever so many snakes. These days he used his arms for stealing copper off the hulls of ships and trolling for bits of the shiny stuff in the brown slop of low tide.

"You *are* an eel," Jake declared. He paused to wipe his face with a corner of his ragged shirt, though I'm not sure why, as both were equally covered in filth. "Slippery and more hard-hearted than most. And that's sayin' a lot, with this 'ere pack of mudlarks."

"I'll take that as a compliment." I grinned.

"Hand it over. You poached on my bit o' river here," Jake said, his voice almost pleading now. "You gotta stay on the edge. Them's the rules, lad."

"You're always goin' on about rules, Jake."

I was bluffing, though, and Jake knew it. In the end, I'd have to give in. A big man like Jake could troll where he wanted. Kids like me had to keep to the edge of the grimy brown river, picking up pieces of coal, rope, rags, and wood at low tide. On a good day, I might collect enough coal to fill a pot and make a penny.

Now that I had my place at the Lion Brewery over on

Broad Street, I'd been mudlarking mostly just in the early mornings, when it was so hot even my stone cellar room seemed about to stifle me. It didn't bring in much, but I needed any extra tin I could get.

"Have a heart, Eel." Jake fixed me with his wild blue eyes and tried again. "Ain't we all riverfinders? Put on this earth to try to get by, one day at a time. We're all we've got under this sky. We need to play fair and take care of one another.

"If I'd known that sooner, I wouldn't have lost sweet Hazel and my kiddies," he went on, almost to himself, slapping the oily surface of the water with his stick.

"All right," I relented at last. "You win. It's yours. Catch!"

The big man lunged and missed, landing flat on his face, sputtering in the churning black water. I laughed and turned to go.

But Jake had the last word.

"You better watch out, Eel!" He rose up, hollering at the top of his lungs. "'E's been nosing around askin' after you, 'e has. Don't blame me—I had nothing to do with it. But 'e says a little birdie told him you ain't dead."

"What?" I froze, digging my feet into the mud. "What did you say?"

"You heard me, lad. You think you're clever, but just you watch out," Jake warned. "I ain't let on I knows anything about you. But Fisheye Bill Tyler is onto you—and a nastier man never walked the streets of London. He might've been an honest fishmonger once. Those days are gone. He's turned bad. Very bad indeed."

"What did he say, Jake?" I demanded.

"Why, Eel, he only wants what's 'is," Jake replied, trying to wipe streaks of dark mud from his grizzled face, this time with his fingers. "Fisheye said he just wants what belongs to 'im by rights."

Jake hadn't touched a hair on my head. But it felt as though he'd knocked the breath right out of me.

"You ain't seen me, Jake," I cried. "You hear me? You know nothin'. All you know is that the Thames got me."

I took a ragged breath, the stink of the river almost making me retch. "You got that? I'm dead, carried out to sea in the arms of this muddy flow. Dead and gone."

"What did you take of 'is, Eel? You must 'ave done something to make 'im that mad," Jake called, holding fast to the scrap of copper he'd finally fished out of the grimy water.

I took off. My insides had begun to shake like the last little leaf on a tree when the cold fingers of a biting wind come to snatch it. *How had he found me out?*

I'd made sure that Fisheye had been told I was dead, swallowed up by the dirty old river, covered by its churning waters. For the last six months, I'd kept low and out of his way. And I'd kept my secret safe.

Until now. How much did Fisheye know? And who had

snitched? It might have been Jake himself. Trust was as rare on the river as finding a gold ring. No, I couldn't trust him.

Thumbless Jake was right about one thing, though. Fish-eye Bill Tyler wanted to control whatever he thought belonged to him—pickpockets, petty thieves, housebreakers.

And me.

CHAPTER TWO
In Which I Save
a Pathetic Creature

I stormed away, sweating, grimy, and wet. You might say I was mired in my own murky thoughts. Next thing I knew, I almost had my head taken off by something hurtling down from the sky—aimed right at me.

"Halloo, Eel," a voice called. "Watch out!"

I jumped back. At first I was afraid the stone arch above me had chosen this day to crumble into the river. Everyone knew Blackfriars Bridge wouldn't last much longer without repairs. But stones didn't screech like the earsplitting sound that filled the air.

Eeeyow!

Splash!

"For you, Eel!"

I looked up. Only one mudlark had orange hair. "What are you torturing now, Ned?"

Before me, the strange creature yowled again, making wild splashes as it struggled to stay afloat. All at once it disappeared. The tide was coming up now, and I lunged, moving into the flow of the river.

"Let it be, why don't you?" Ned hollered with cruel delight. "Let's see if it can swim."

I tried to scoop the creature out. It lashed at me, hard. "Ouch! That was my arm."

I almost left it to drown. I didn't fancy getting scratched to shreds and having my arms turn bright red from dirty wounds. Last winter, another mudlark, a lad of only eight, had nearly lost his foot after stepping on a piece of sharp glass.

Then I remembered my old muslin bag, which I used for carrying odd bits of rope and pieces of coal. Maybe I could catch the creature in that.

"C'mon now," I urged, slipping the bag off my shoulder and holding it out with both hands.

At first it splashed and squealed and fought something fierce. I couldn't get near it. Then it disappeared under the oily surface again. In a flash I reached below and scooped the sodden creature up into my bag. "Gotcha!"

Wading to the riverbank, I held the bag tight against my body and peered inside. A pair of bright green eyes—green as a queen's emeralds—stared back at me out of a mass of bedraggled black fur.

I grinned. "You fight hard for such a scrawny animal. Now be still and I'll rub you dry. You should be grateful I came along when I did, Little Queenie."

I looked up to see Ned still leaning over the side of the bridge. "You are a nasty one. What'd you wanna do that for?"

"Aw, don't go soft on me, Eel. It was just a bit of mischief."

A bit of mischief. I wondered what other mischief Ned had been up to lately. Maybe he'd been the one to betray me to Fisheye. Ned could probably be bought for the price of a hot meat pie or a pint of cider.

In my arms the tiny cat shivered. Then, as if suddenly realizing she was safe, she tried to bury herself under the crook of my elbow.

"Ah, Little Queenie, take my advice and don't trust boys—or anyone," I told her, wrapping the bag around her more snugly and tucking her under my arm. "Luckily, you're safe with me. I'm taking you back to the Lion, where you can start earning your keep catchin' rats. I felt one ticklin' my toes just the other night."

For answer, she began to purr.

On my way back to the Lion, I passed through Covent Garden, where the flower sellers were just setting up their stalls. Clutches of girls were busy tying violets into bunches, laughing and gossiping as they worked. The streets were already a bustle of carts and wagons piled high with vegetables, chickens, cheese, and fruit from the countryside.

The smell of frying fish, potatoes, and onions drifted toward me, making my stomach growl. It brought me back to last winter, when just the smell of frying onions could make me almost faint with hunger.

Then I relaxed and smiled a little. Those days were gone. I had a situation now, a good one. When I got back to Broad Street, I would have bread, cheese, and a cool dipper of good water waiting for me in my tiny corner in the cellar of the Lion Brewery.

I moved quickly, my cap pulled low, my old shoes squelching on the cobblestones. I'd let my guard down these last few months since I'd come to the Lion. Jake's words were a warning: I needed to keep a sharp lookout from now on. Fisheye had spies everywhere: pickpockets mostly, and the gang of petty thieves who did his dirty work for him.

He won't think to look for me on Broad Street, or anywhere else near the Golden Square park in Soho, I tried to convince myself as I headed north. Fisheye didn't frequent that neighborhood much. He would expect me to be keeping low in the crowded slums—we called them rookeries—of Southwark, south of the river.

And he won't find what I've hidden. I had to make sure of that. That's what mattered most.

The little cat squirmed and clawed every time a horse neighed or a dog barked close by. Sometimes she held her tiny mouth on my arm and bit hard. "Stop it or I'll let you down under the wheels of the next cart," I warned.

But, of course, I never would.

I was about to cross Broad Street to the Lion Brewery when I spotted the white face of Mrs. Lewis staring up at me from the open window of her cellar. "Hullo, Mrs. Lewis. Baby wake you early?"

"Before it was light. Poor Fanny. The wee thing has it comin' out both ends." She nodded at the bucket she held, which she'd just finished dumping in the cesspool in the cellar.

Through the window, I could see that the cesspool—that deep, smelly pit where all the chamber pots were emptied—was almost full. Time for the night-soil men to come round and empty it. Thumbless Jake had told me he'd once done a stint as a night-soil man.

"That life weren't for me, Eel," he said with a shake of his head. "I heard of one poor lad who fell in a cesspool and couldn't get out. Nasty way to die, that was. Now, I know this old river don't smell like roses, but at least out here I got the sky above me."

Mrs. Lewis put her bucket down and sighed. "If it keeps up, I might call round for the doctor."

"Dr. Snow?" I asked.

Her brows knit. "I never heard of him. We call Dr. William Rogers when we needs a doctor."

"Dr. Snow lives on Sackville Street. He's a smart one, Mrs. Lewis. I've been tending his animals all summer," I said, unable to keep the pride from my voice. "He's what you call a real scientist. Does all sorts of experiments."

"You don't say?"

"Dr. Snow has learned to put animals—and even people—to sleep for short periods of time with a special gas, so as they won't feel pain," I explained. "He made a grizzly bear that needed a tooth pulled go to sleep, and even eased the queen's pain when she gave birth to Prince Leopold last year."

"If he's doctoring giant grizzlies and Queen Victoria herself, he must be a clever one." She wiped her forehead with the tip of her apron and picked up her bucket. "Well, I'd best be getting back upstairs before Fanny wakes."

"Give my regards to Constable Lewis," I said politely. "And I hope Annie Ribbons don't get sick."

"Is that what you call my girl?" Mrs. Lewis smiled. "She do like to collect ribbons and threads, I'll say that. She's already a better seamstress than me. But, goodness, you children and your nicknames! Seems like no child around the Golden Square ever gets called by 'is true name.'"

Mrs. Lewis put a hand to her back, as though it ached, which it probably did on account of the buckets she carried from the second floor down to the cellar. "I've always been curious, Eel. What's your real name?"

I grinned. "I'll never tell, Mrs. Lewis."

And I wouldn't. Especially now that Fisheye could be closin' in on me. More than ever, I had to be like an eel.

I said goodbye and turned on my heel to head across the street.

"Eel! Watch where you're goin', you clumsy lad!" Florrie Baker jumped aside, but I had to reach out and steady myself on the Broad Street pump to keep from sprawling to the cobblestones. I squeezed Little Queenie tight to keep from dropping her.

"Sorry." I grinned into the second pair of green eyes I'd seen that morning. Though I wasn't about to tell Florrie Baker she had anything in common with a half-drowned cat—not if I wanted to avoid getting knocked down for real. "You're up early. Fetchin' water for your mum?"

"That I am." She wrinkled her nose. "You been at the river, ain't you? You got the stink of the Thames about you. And whatever is making your bag wriggle like that?"

Just then a freckle-faced boy came up behind Florrie, leading a pony and a small cart. He stopped and cleared his throat. "Beggin' your pardon, Florrie. Can I have a turn at the pump? I need to get to Hampstead and back this morning."

"Go right ahead, Gus, unless Eel here wants a turn first," said Florrie. She picked up her bucket and moved aside.

"Not me. At the Lion we get water delivered from the

New River Company, and we have our own well," I said, pushing the cat more firmly under my arm so she wouldn't wriggle so much. "Besides, I like the Warwick Street pump water better. Can't say exactly why."

Gus stepped up to fill his jug, not taking his eyes off Florrie. I jabbed her in the ribs and whispered, "One of your admirers?"

Florrie giggled. "Now don't you say anything against Gus. 'E's a steady boy—has a job as a runner at the Eley Brothers factory down the street. And thoughtful too. Even brings me flowers sometimes."

Flowers? Was Florrie the sort of girl who liked flowers? The most I'd ever given her was a pencil.

Florrie stepped closer and tried to peer into my bag. "Now let's see what you got in here."

I peeled the bag open to reveal the little cat's wet head. Florrie laughed. "So, are you rescuin' kittens now, or is this creature for that famous Dr. Snow you're always goin' on about?"

"Dr. Snow mostly keeps guinea pigs, mice, frogs, and rabbits these days," I told her. "I'm gonna raise Little Queenie up as a ratter at the Lion."

I paused. "Unless . . . that is . . . maybe you'd like her."

Florrie grinned. "Our Jasper would claw her pretty face to pieces. Besides, we can't take on another mouth to feed, even a cat. Mum has her hands full trying to feed a family of five. "I'm goin' to be helpin' Mum out, though, soon enough." She looked serious now. "It's been settled. I'm to go into service in a fortnight."

"You are? But where?"

"Worried you won't see me ever?" she teased. "Don't fret. I'll be working for a nice lady and her elderly father in North London, not too far away. Close enough to walk home on my half day off to see all my old friends."

"What will you do?"

"Where do all girls start? I'm to be the scullery maid. But before long, mark my words, I'll be housemaid in charge of everything," she told me confidently. "I'm twelve, after all, thirteen come next winter. It's time I did my part."

"So . . . so I guess this means you'll leave the ragged school?"

"I was lucky to go this long. Nancy only went to school till she was ten." She pulled a small, dog-eared sketchbook from her pocket and giggled. "I'll draw you pictures of all the fancy dishes the fine folks eat."

I grinned, though I wondered if she'd have time for that. I'd seen scullery maids, their hands swollen and red from all that washing up. "Maybe you can sketch Little Queenie for me someday. Once she's properly dried off, that is."

"I will," she promised, slipping her sketchbook back into her pocket.

Across the way, the front door of the Lion opened. The business day was starting.

"I'd best get this little one somethin' to nibble on before

I start work," I told Florrie. "Don't want to be late or I'll catch trouble."

"Can I come feed Dr. Snow's animals with you today?" she asked. "I haven't seen them yet, and soon I won't have the chance."

"Meet me here later," I agreed. "I can't go until I'm done with work at the Lion and sweepin' up for Mr. Griggs."

"I swear, Eel, you're the busiest lad in Soho," said Florrie. "What do you do with all your extra tin? You certainly don't use it to buy clothes."

Florrie was my best friend. Only friend, really. But I hadn't even told her why I needed money, or why I didn't ever get clothes or treats for myself.

"Florrie, here's something I *would* like to do with my money," I said suddenly. "I'd like to buy you an Italian ice."

The chance to see Florrie Baker smile was definitely worth a penny.

CHAPTER THREE
Thief!

Thursday, August 31

"It's like breathin' soup," Abel Cooper complained, same as he had every morning for a week. "Hot, stinkin' soup."

"Any errands for later, Mr. Cooper?" I asked the foreman as I mopped the brewery floor.

"In this heat? No, I'll not send you out. There's bad air out there. Poison," he declared, wiping his forehead. "Bad air brings trouble."

"What kind of trouble, sir?"

"Disease, lad. Since ancient times, folks have known that bad air—what they call miasma—is the cause of disease. And that's what we've got now: noxious, poisonous air. It smells like . . . well, you know."

I did. We all did. "Mr. Cooper, exactly which diseases does miasma cause?"

"You name it: measles, scarlet fever, smallpox, and, worst of all, the blue death," he answered. "It's obvious when you think on it, ain't it? Bad smells cause bad things."

I nodded, though I wondered how it was that Thumbless Jake, Ned, and the rest of the mudlarks were still walking around. Seemed like we all should be laid low by now from inhaling that filthy, smelly air that rose off the Thames. Especially since so much of London's garbage and human and animal waste got dumped into it.

As for the heat, well, that didn't bother me so much. I had too many bad memories of winter, with its tentacles of icy fog that bite into you and won't let go. But there was no denying it was hot. Hot from dawn till dark. And not a dry heat, like you find in an oven. No, it was hot in a thick, wet sort of way, as if the sun were a giant who'd aimed his moist, stinky breath on us all.

The whole city reeked of fish, rotten fruit, horse droppings, and worse. The thick, foul air stung our eyes. Each morning the sky turned a murky yellow. That was day. It stayed that way till, hours later, the sickly yellow sky faded away to a hot, muddy gray. That was night.

Even deep in the cellar of the Lion Brewery, where the stone walls made things a bit cooler, I sometimes saw Little Queenie panting, her tiny pink tongue sticking out. She'd settled in well, though. Small as she was, she'd already delivered a mouse, purring with pride as she laid it at my feet.

"Next time, go for the rats, Li'l Queenie," I instructed. "Them's the nasty ones that crawl over me at night, their long, snaky tails ticklin' my skin. You're a big girl now—take 'em on."

Mr. Cooper was a regular brick—if he could spare us messenger boys from traipsing all over in the horrible, stinking heat, he did. And maybe that's why it happened. Maybe it had something to do with us being so cooped up. I can't say for sure. What I do know is that if I'd thought my troubles were over for the week, I was gravely mistaken.

I'd finished mopping and was dumping the bucket in the courtyard when Hugzie Huggins tapped me on the shoulder. *Pushed* would be a better way to say it. I stumbled, sloshing water over my legs.

"Watch it!" I felt like knocking him flat.

"You're wanted, Eel."

My stomach lurched. Herbert "Hugzie" Huggins was the nephew of the Lion's owners, the Huggins brothers—John and Edward. Hugzie had a pumpkin-shaped head and grimy yellow hair. He smelled of onions and burps. I'd always wondered how he'd gotten that nickname. A less huggable lad I never saw.

"Who wants me?"

"My uncle does."

"Mr. Edward?" I asked hopefully. Mr. Edward was my favorite. He was a fair man who cared about his workers. As for his older brother, I made it my business to stay out of his way.

"Uncle John needs to see you," Hugzie said. He couldn't keep the sneer off his face. "Mr. John Huggins to you."

"What about?" I snapped, suddenly suspicious. Something didn't feel right. "I been doin' my job. Workin' harder than you."

Hugzie just shrugged, his plump lips twitching as though he was trying not to laugh. What was he up to? As I followed him up the passageway to the office, I tried to stay calm. *I'll be able to handle whatever he doles out,* I told myself. *After all, I can hold my own with Thumbless Jake.*

Maybe I was just extra jittery, on account of what Thumbless Jake had let on about Fisheye. Or maybe Abel Cooper's talk about the bad air carrying poison was getting to me. But I couldn't keep from feeling like I was headed for something dark and unknown. It was a little like wading into the deepest part of the river at high tide, without even a lantern in my hand.

Mr. John Huggins was all business. He sat ramrod straight behind a large oak desk, surrounded by tall stacks of papers. I stared at the battered tin box in the center of his desk. I felt a hot flush of anger stain my cheeks.

"That's mine! You weasel—you've been in my things." I whirled on Hugzie and grabbed his shirt.

Hugzie squealed like a piglet. "Uncle, get him off!"

"Stop that," commanded Mr. John, though I'd already pulled away.

Watch your temper, I reminded myself.

Mum's warnings came back to me: "Try to be more like your grandpa. He was the mildest man I ever knew. He always said the best way to win an argument is to pretend you're pouring cool water on a hot fire." But I didn't take after my grandpa.

Mr. John had tiny, glittery eyes just like his nephew. But mostly it was his eyebrows you noticed. They grew up out of his forehead like a thicket of branches.

"Don't turn on young Herbert here," he purred, though it was not the same purr as Little Queenie's sweet, contented sound. It was more like a lion's menacing growl, or at least what I imagined a lion might sound like. "Herbert is quite correct to bring this to my attention."

He gestured to the box on his desk. "Now, young man, can you tell me where these coins came from?"

"They're . . . they're mine . . . ," I spluttered stupidly.

"I think you know that stealing is grounds for instant dismissal," Mr. John said coldly.

That is exactly what Hugzie wants, I realized with a start. *He's trying to get rid of me.*

My heart sank. My eyes burned with tears I wouldn't let fall. This couldn't be happening. I'd been safe here at the

Lion since May. I had food, clean water, and a place to sleep. Abel Cooper treated all of us messenger boys fairly.

I couldn't be thrown back on the streets. Not now, with Fisheye Bill looking for me. I dreaded taking up the life of a mudlark again, scavenging in the filthy river day after day, no matter what the weather. Being a street sweeper wasn't much better: pushing aside dog and horse dung from the paths of gents and ladies, then standing by and hoping for tuppence. It was little better than begging.

These last few months at the Lion had changed things for me. I'd started to believe I could make something of myself someday. I might be a foreman like Abel Cooper, or maybe I could start a small shop, learn a trade, or even become a clerk, just as Pa had been.

All this was far off. What mattered now was protecting my secret. And to keep it safe, I needed four shillings a week. Four shillings and a penny, to be exact, to be delivered each Friday. That was the precise amount I had in my box—all ready for tomorrow morning. And except for a few coins in my pocket, it was all I had in the world.

"I earned this money fairly, sir," I declared. "I do odd jobs at night or when I'm not needed here."

"What kind of odd jobs?"

"I feed animals and clean their cages for a doctor over on Sackville Street. And when I'm done here in the evening, I help Mr. Griggs, the tailor who has a shop across the road, at Number Forty," I explained. "I sweep up the extra threads and bits of cloth, and make it tidy for customers the next morning. You can ask Mr. Griggs yourself."

"Now, young man, no need to get excited," Mr. John said in that same cool, smooth tone. He picked up a small ivory-handled penknife and began running the blade under his fingernails.

He's enjoying this, I thought. *He likes making me squirm.*

"I find your story somewhat suspicious," he said slowly, still concentrating on his nails as though he couldn't even be bothered to look at me. "Do you really have time and energy at the end of the day to hire yourself out to someone else? Surely Mr. Cooper can find more work for you if that is the case."

I clenched and unclenched my fists. "I always check with Mr. Cooper, sir, before I go. He'll tell you I'm a good worker."

I almost let slip that I was sure Mr. Edward would back me up too. But that might not help me with Mr. John. Suddenly I remembered something. Just yesterday I'd come around a corner and heard Mr. Edward's voice. "Don't let it happen again, Herbert."

I hadn't thought much about it then. Now I wondered: had Mr. Edward caught Hugzie skimming pennies off a payment?

When Hugzie and I were sent to collect on a bill, we were supposed to return with the correct amount of money. But it *was* possible to cheat—to say that the customer hadn't been happy with his lot of brew and had kept back a shilling, or that the customer had shorted us and we hadn't noticed. Maybe Mr. Edward had discovered that Hugzie had come up short too many times.

"Let me ask you another question," Mr. John was saying, switching the little knife from one hand to the other and starting to dig into the skin behind his thumbnail. I watched, unable to take my eyes off the shining tip of that tiny blade.

That's what I am to him, I thought. *Just a speck of troublesome dirt under a nail.*

"You claim you earned this money through your own labor. But what possible reason do you have? Are you not satisfied with your job here at the Lion? You get room and board and good water to drink. What use do you have for extra money?" Mr. John demanded.

I couldn't tell him the truth, of course. I thought fast.

"To better meself, sir," I said meekly, lowering my gaze to the tips of my old shoes. I could see my left toe beginning to poke out. It would take more than one sweep of Mr. John's penknife to get *my* nails clean. "I'd like to, uh . . . make sure I have proper shoes, so as to look presentable when I deliver messages and suchlike."

Mr. John waved a hand, as though to clear the air of my words. "Are you aware, young man, that there have been some irregularities in the accounts here?"

I whirled around to look at Hugzie and caught the tiniest of smiles flittering on his puffy lips. My hunch was right: Hugzie had been skimming the odd coin from his uncles' operation. When he'd found my box, he figured this was a chance to put the blame on me.

I lowered my head again, feeling trapped. *If only Mr. Edward were here.* But Mr. Edward was gone on business all week. Hugzie had chosen his moment carefully. He wasn't quite as stupid as he looked: he must have seen that Mr. Edward watched out for me. I wondered if Hugzie had resented me from the beginning. For it was Mr. Edward himself who'd agreed to let Abel Cooper take me on at the Lion.

Of course, I had Thumbless Jake to thank too. It was the nicest thing Jake had ever done. It had happened one raw, cold night in early spring, when it seemed like winter wouldn't ever let go. Jake had stood me a mutton pie in a pub on the Strand that night. "You look like a drowned rat," he'd growled as the rain beat down on us.

As we'd sat steaming in front of a fire, the rest of the patrons keeping their distance (not surprising, given the way we smelled), Abel Cooper had walked in and recognized Thumbless Jake.

"Why, if it ain't Jake!" he exclaimed cheerily, coming over to shake Jake's hand. "Remember me from the Lion? You used to shoe all the horses for our delivery wagons. Let me buy you a pint. I was that sorry to hear you'd left the business. I still say you were the best smith in London. Is this your lad here?"

"I'll take a gin, Abel, if it's all the same to you," Jake muttered, his eyes lowered. Even through the layer of dirt on his skin, I could see a pink flush of shame creep up his neck.

Poor Jake, I remember thinking. *It's not easy for him to see his old pal now that he's so down on his luck.*

Maybe it was Jake feeling like he wanted to be in charge of *something* that made him put me forward. "This is Eel," he told Abel Cooper. "Now, 'e ain't my boy, but 'e's a good lad nonetheless. Had some letterin' too. I hate to see 'im waste away on the river. You got a use for a boy over at the Lion?"

Abel Cooper looked me up and down. "You seem a sharp lad, with those dark, bright eyes," he said agreeably. "Are you willing to work hard, boy?"

"Oh, yes, sir."

"Well, then, if you can clean yerself up, lad, so you don't carry the stink of the Thames with you, I'll have you meet Mr. Edward Huggins," said Mr. Cooper. "Business is due to pick up this spring, and we could use a new messenger boy and someone to mop the floors and clean the place."

"Thank you, sir."

"You'll have to pass muster with Mr. Edward, of course, but he's a kind gentleman, not a bit like his brother," Abel Cooper said. "Come to Broad Street in two weeks, lad. And get yourself cleaned up."

That's how I landed my position at the Lion Brewery. It was also why I owed Jake.

* * *

I'd done all right at the Lion, making myself useful and working hard for my keep. I fetched meat pies from the street sellers for the higher-ups. Seeing as how I knew London streets like the back of my hand, I could always be depended on to deliver messages quick-like. Part of the day, I'd sit in the Boys' Box, a small room with a counter and pigeonholes and bells. Whenever a bell rang, I'd leap into action. I'd deliver the message as fast as I could and run right back for the next one.

I hadn't been there long before Abel Cooper remarked on my speed. "How'd you get back so fast?" he asked me once when I turned up not long after going way over to Doughty Street. "The other messenger boys are constantly getting lost. It's like you've got a map of the city in your head."

I thought about this for a minute. "Well, Mr. Cooper, in a way I do. I've walked a lot, and know my way around the city. I make a map in my head before I start. So I usually can get there and back right quick."

I'd been this way since I was little. Seeing how things fit together seemed to come natural.

"You're like your father," Mum had said once. I did have memories, thin and dreamlike, of long walks with Pa, or of sitting on his lap as he pored over a giant map of London, spread out to cover the entire table.

Abel Cooper had been pleased with my response. "Well done, Eel. I'll mention this to Mr. Edward."

Now Hugzie was trying to take all this away from me. I had to find a way to change Mr. John's mind.

"Sir, if you want proof of where the extra coins in this tin box are from, let me fetch Mr. Griggs the tailor," I said. "He'll vouch for me."

Mr. John hesitated, and I felt sure he'd say no. Then he relented.

"All right," he said reluctantly. "Ask Mr. Griggs to step over here if he is free. Let's see if you're telling the truth."

"But . . . but, Uncle, he's guilty!" Hugzie protested.

I was already pushing past him. I had a second chance.

After sprinting across the cobblestoned street, I stood in front of the tailor shop. No family on Broad Street had their own house. The Griggs family lived in two rooms above the shop. Constable Lewis and his wife and children crammed into a single room on the same floor.

Conditions were even worse in other poor neighborhoods. I'd spent nights crouched in doorways in tiny, crowded courtyards teeming with barefoot children and crying babies. It didn't seem a fit place for humans to live.

At least Broad Street had a good number of shops, and we were close to a spot of grass in Golden Square.

I was already thinking of what I would say to Mr. Griggs. But as soon as I pulled open the door, I knew something was wrong.

CHAPTER FOUR
Mr. Griggs the Tailor

Something had changed in the tailor shop. First off, it was quiet. It appeared empty too. It felt so eerie, little hairs on my arms began to prickle and stand up all on their own.

Mr. Griggs was nowhere in sight. That wasn't like him. The busy tailor was almost always at work, rarely stopping even to eat during the day. "Folks don't pay me to put grease on their jackets," he'd once told me with a hearty laugh. "I leave that to them."

Mr. Griggs was devoted to his trade. He liked to greet his customers, fresh and pleasant-like, even if he'd already seen them twice since breakfast. He treated me the same way. "Eel! How nice to see you," he'd say each evening.

"Dear boy, I've made a fearful mess for you to sweep up today."

Now, as my eyes grew used to the shadows, I saw that the shop wasn't deserted, after all: five-year-old Bernie and his sister, Betsy, two years older, were there. Bernie and Betsy were usually as rambunctious as kittens. But here they were, posed as prim and stiff as a little gentleman and miss, on the chairs reserved for customers.

I had an odd feeling looking at them, a stab of memory. They reminded me of a time when I'd hoped that if I was extra, extra good and didn't move a muscle, I could keep something bad from happening.

Bernie's face had streaks of dirt and tears on it. Betsy had her hands tucked under her. Her black-and-white runt of a dog lay curled by her chair. Dilly swished her tail lazy-like when she spotted me, but even she was being extra well behaved: most days she'd jump up and twirl like a spinning top.

Mr. Griggs sometimes called her Silly Dilly. "Where's my welcome, Dilly girl?" he liked to say. Dilly had followed Mr. Griggs home from Piccadilly Circus one day. We figured she'd come into the city on a farmer's cart and gotten separated from her master in that great, bustling intersection, which was always packed with horses, carts, and crowds.

"Poor wee pup. How could I resist bringin' her home to Betsy?" Mr. Griggs said. He was convinced that Dilly was the smartest dog in London. "If I hadn't picked her up, I don't doubt she would've found her way back to the farm she was born on. But now she loves us too much to go anywhere, ain't that right, Miss Piccadilly?" I'd almost made the mistake of pointing out that if Dilly had had such a keen sense of direction, she wouldn't have gotten lost in the first place.

Not everyone in London took kindly to dogs as pets, but Dilly's family treated her like royalty. She was especially fond of sausage rolls. I even found myself buying one for her sometimes. I'd feed it to her in small bits, which drove her so crazy she'd sit at my feet, throw up her muzzle to the sky, and howl.

I went over and scratched behind Dilly's soft ears. In a low voice I asked Betsy, "So where's your father, then?"

"Pa ain't feeling well," Betsy whispered. "Mum says I should tell everyone that he begs you to please return another day."

I couldn't do that! I needed to talk to Mr. Griggs—now. If he didn't speak up for me in the next hour, I might find myself sleeping in an upturned boat by the side of the Thames tonight.

I stared at the children, unsure what to do. Tears pooled up in Bernie's eyes and ran down his cheeks. He thrust his fists against his face as if trying to make them stop.

I looked to Betsy. "Was it somethin' he ate?"

She nodded, swallowing hard. "Pa's stomach hurts somethin' awful and he's real thirsty."

I frowned. It might be nothing. Stomach upsets were to be expected, especially in summer. Maybe I could just slip upstairs for a quick word. Mr. Griggs might be well enough to jot a brief note to Mr. John on my behalf.

"Well, I'll just go up and poke my head in at the door. Your ma might need me to fetch something from the coster-monger." Fishing into my pocket, I drew out two halfpenny coins, almost all the money I had left. "I saw an Italian ice man and his cart on the corner of Berwick Street. Go on and get yourselves a lemon ice."

Betsy and Bernie sprang up, grabbed the coins, and ran out, their bare feet pattering on the wooden floorboards. I made my way up the narrow staircase. It was hard to breathe. The air was stale and hot. Yet, for some reason, a shiver ran down my spine.

It's just nerves after what's happened at the Lion, I told myself. *Don't be daft.*

It might be rude to barge in like this, but if I lost my situation and ended up back on the street, my chances of keeping out of Fisheye's way weren't good. I'd be no use to anyone who needed me then. No use at all.

And someone *did* need me.

The door ahead of me was slightly ajar. I gave it a gentle push with my foot. It creaked and swung open. Mrs. Griggs, a neat, plain woman with a gentle face, startled at the noise.

"Pardon me, Mrs. Griggs . . . ," I began.

Then I stopped.

I stopped for a long, terrible minute, unable to breathe or think or even understand the scene before me. What I saw was this: Mr. Griggs lay in a corner of the small room, resting on a pile of sheets. Well, I don't suppose you could call it resting. Far from it. For in truth, he looked to be in pure agony.

I'm sure my mouth was wide open in shock. I thought to close it, and just as I did, Mr. Griggs clutched his belly and started to writhe, back and forth, back and forth, something awful. His blond hair looked almost black with sweat.

Then there were the sounds he made. From deep in his throat came small, horrible cries of pain. There was a chamber pot nearby. And some extra buckets. But I don't think he'd had the strength to use them.

The sheets under the tailor were covered with what looked like water. At first I figured Mrs. Griggs had tried to cool off his fever. But then I saw that it wasn't water at all, but strange masses of tiny white particles, like rice. Something pricked at the back of my mind. *White particles . . . white particles.*

I'd heard something about them before, somewhere. But what?

"Oh, Eel, lad. You oughtn't to be here. Didn't Betsy tell you?" Mrs. Griggs said in a fierce, urgent whisper. "He's been exploding . . . the pain . . . I sent the children downstairs. You go too. Go now."

"Mrs. Griggs, do you . . . do you need anything?"

She stared at me helplessly, as if I'd spoken in a foreign language.

"Don't you understand?" she hissed softly. "There's nothing you can do. . . ."

Her voice trailed off. Mr. Griggs cried out and she rushed over. After that she seemed to forget I was there.

I swallowed hard. I thought I would throw up, and I might have if I'd stayed any longer. Instead I left. Fast. I backed out of the room and clattered down the stairway without drawing a breath. In a second I was out into the street.

I stood quivering, taking in great gasps of air that was so sticky it hardly counted as air at all. And there, right across the cobblestones, stood the Lion Brewery.

I'm lost now, I thought. *I'll never get my job back. There's not even any sense in goin' back inside. I'll have to put up with Mr. John dismissing me—and hope he doesn't have me put in jail as a thief.*

I shouldn't be thinking of myself first, I knew, with Mr. Griggs suffering so. Then I remembered what I'd heard about those white particles. That's what came out of people when they fell sick with the cholera.

Mr. Griggs had been struck down by the blue death.

CHAPTER FIVE
Urchins on Excursion

I stood there, frozen with horror, for at least ten minutes. *What next?* Behind me, up in that room, was Mr. Griggs. In front of me was the Lion. And looming up around every corner was the shadow of Fisheye Bill Tyler.

"Bad air brings trouble," Abel Cooper had warned. It seemed he was right. But how could so much trouble happen in just a few days?

I couldn't do much for Mr. Griggs. And unless I wanted to hide in a London sewer and never come out, I'd have to take my chances that Fisheye might find me. I needed my situation at the Lion (and my four shillings!) back. The only other person who might help me was Dr. John Snow.

Or would he? Even though I took care of Dr. Snow's

animals every night when I was done sweeping the tailor shop, I rarely saw the doctor himself. He was either out on a call or attending some important meeting or dinner. I tried to avoid the stern Mrs. Weatherburn, his housekeeper, except when it was time to get paid. Still, it was worth a try.

It might be the only chance I have left, I thought.

I was about to set off when Florrie Baker came storming toward me, buzzing like an angry fly. "Eel! Is this your doing?"

"What are you talking about?" Then I saw.

Behind Florrie were three dirty, wailing kids. Betsy and Bernie came first, sniffling and gulping. Bernie must have scraped his knee; trickles of blood ran down his leg. Annie Lewis, who'd tied bits of thread and ribbons around her wrist, tagged behind.

Woof! Woof!

Adding to the confusion was Dilly. She dashed in circles around the crying children. Every once in a while, she caught sight of her own tail and began to chase it. When she couldn't catch it, she barked harder.

"Dilly, shush!" Florrie scolded. She turned to me, hands on her hips. "Annie and I found these two cryin' over by the Golden Square, all turned around. Bernie fell and nearly got trampled by a horse and cart."

"It was a giant horse," Betsy reported. "I thought Bernie would get smashed flat."

"They said you sent them off," Florrie continued. "Eel,

they're no more than babies! You know their pa likes to keep them close."

"The horse was giant! A black monster." Bernie gave a huge hiccup, his face stained with dirty tears. Then he remembered the most important thing. "We couldn't find the ice man. I want my ice. You promised."

"Me too," Betsy begged, tugging at my shirt. "And I want to see the doctor's animals. Florrie said you'd take us."

I glared at Florrie, who shrugged. "We may as well bring them all and give their mums a break."

"Aw, Florrie, think how it'll look. It ain't . . . business-like," I protested. "I got . . . I got something I need to discuss with Dr. Snow."

"Look at you, all puffed up just 'cause you take care of animals for some swell doctor." Florrie sniffed. "It ain't like you work for the queen herself. They won't be any trouble."

I shook my head and grumbled, "You're all trouble!"

Florrie put her hands on her hips, waiting for me to give in. Florrie was stubborn. She was also the closest thing I had to a best friend. But still, I hadn't told her about the blue death, or about Mr. Huggins accusing me of being a thief.

They all watched me. Even Dilly stared up at me expectantly. I gave in at last. "All right, all right. But you've got to stay close and keep up."

"I'll run in and let Mrs. Griggs know," Florrie offered, moving toward the tailor's shop.

"No, I'll go." I put out a hand to stop her. "It ain't good for my reputation if I'm left standing here on the road like a nursemaid."

I ran back inside and up a few steps. I yelled out to Mrs. Lewis and Mrs. Griggs that their little ones were safe with Florrie and me. I didn't wait for an answer. I didn't want to go back into that room. Not unless I had to.

"So, Bernie, tell me," said Florrie as we walked along. "What's your favorite ice? Mine's raspberry."

"Lemon," he said. "Pa likes strawberry."

"How about you, Betsy?" I asked.

Betsy didn't answer. Her face was pinched and white, almost as if she might be sick herself. She tripped and I grabbed her hand.

Regent Street was a bustle of cabs, horses, hawkers calling out their wares, and crowds of people. I looked behind me. "Keep up, Annie Ribbons!"

"I am. I just had to look at the pretty hats in that window," she squeaked. Annie was nearly nine, but she was as scrawny as a six-year-old. That's how it was in our neighborhood. Mr. Lewis might be a constable, but that didn't mean it was easy to feed a family.

Constable Lewis. I wondered if he would stand up for me with Mr. John Huggins. But that could be dangerous. If Constable Lewis knew the whole truth, there was a chance

I could be put in the St. James Workhouse. I was too much like Thumbless Jake for that: I wanted the sky overhead.

"Watch out!" I pulled Betsy back from a cart that came so close the mare jerked her head in alarm.

"Slow down, Eel!" Florrie panted, trying to keep up and dragging Bernie behind her. "What's put you in such a bad temper? We're supposed to be having fun!"

I scowled and pulled them off into a side street. It was quieter here. I let out my breath and felt the tension drain away a little. Fisheye could have pickpockets at work in busy crowds most anywhere, but we would be safe in this neighborhood.

Florrie sent the little ones ahead. "So what's wrong?" she wanted to know. "Has something happened at the Lion?"

"What makes you say that?"

"Well, for one thing, it's the middle of the day and you're not at work," Florrie pointed out. "And for another, you're as bristly as the needles on one of Annie's pincushions."

"Mr. John Huggins thinks I'm a thief," I admitted.

"Was it Hugzie who got you in trouble?"

I nodded. "He snuck into my things, took my money, and tried to convince his uncle I'd stolen it. Now I've probably lost my place."

I stopped, not wanting to spill the whole story of my secret box. "How did you guess Hugzie had something to do with it?"

Florrie snorted. "You've never tried to hide that you're smarter than him. He's the nephew of the owners, after all."

"I thought you'd be on my side."

"I am. I'm just saying, those of us on the bottom got to be careful." Florrie touched me gently on the shoulder. "Have you asked Mr. Griggs to help? He must know Mr. Huggins."

I hesitated. "Mr. Griggs . . . wasn't feeling well enough to see me." I almost told her everything—that the tailor most likely had been struck with the blue death. But this wasn't the time, what with Betsy and Bernie so close. Besides, maybe if I put it off, it wouldn't be true.

Florrie was silent a moment. Then she said, as if the idea had just come into her mind, "Eel, you told me Hugzie took your money. What money? What have you been saving money for?"

I shrugged. "Nothing much."

"You know, sometimes when I ask you things, it's like you don't want to answer." Florrie fixed me with her clear, honest gaze. "And when you do, it's like you're trying to sell me fish that's gone off a bit and you think I can't smell it."

Then she sprinted ahead to pick up Bernie, who'd fallen down again. I was left to walk alone and think about her words.

By the time we got to Sackville Street, with its clean stone town houses all lined up in a neat row, Annie, Bernie, and Betsy were wide-eyed. "It's so quiet. Almost like bein' in St. Luke's," Betsy breathed.

"Nice, ain't it? This is where the swells live," Florrie explained. To me she said, "I'll be working in a fine house like this soon."

"Dr. Snow lives in Number Eighteen," I said, pointing to a house with a large door and with four windows on all three floors. I still couldn't quite believe that someone as important as Dr. Snow trusted me—a mudlark—to look after his animals.

"Your doctor has this *whole* house to himself?" asked Betsy, craning her neck to see the upper floors.

I nodded proudly. "'Course he does. Dr. John Snow is quite a gentleman. So be on your best conduct in his yard or there won't be any ices on the way home."

I jerked my head. "Now follow me. We need to go around the back way, through the alley. Mrs. Jane Weatherburn, Dr. Snow's housekeeper, leaves newspapers and food scraps out there for me to use."

"How did you meet Dr. Snow?" Florrie asked.

"In Covent Garden. He came to the market to buy a guinea pig," I said. "You know how busy and noisy it is there. Just as Dr. Snow was putting the guinea pig into a little box to take it home, a horse spooked behind him, toppling a cart of vegetables and making a terrible racket. Well, the guinea pig got such a fright it squirmed out of Dr. Snow's grasp. Luckily, I happened to be standing right there to catch it."

They were all watching me now, and I continued the

story, holding up my hands as though cupping an invisible guinea pig. "'Here, sir, let me help you. I'm good with animals. My name is Eel, so I know exactly how these creatures think when they're trying to wriggle away.'"

"You gave it back to 'im, then?" Bernie asked, sounding disappointed.

I nodded. "Before you know it, I had it safe in its little carrying box."

"Then he offered you the job?" Betsy asked.

"Weren't quite as easy as all that. I had a trial period first, to prove myself," I recalled. "And not just to Dr. Snow, but to Mrs. Weatherburn too. She's like a general. Inspected my work for three weeks before she gave me the nod."

She had also given me a warning: "Boy, if I catch you taking advantage of Dr. Snow's generous nature, I'll be getting the constable after you, and don't think I won't."

Now I looked around warily. *Should I have brought Florrie and the little ones here at all?* I wouldn't want Mrs. Weatherburn to think we were a gang of thieves.

I could just imagine her bursting out the back door, holding her broom high and shouting, "Scat!"

CHAPTER SIX
Dr. Snow's Menagerie

I let myself into Dr. Snow's backyard through the black iron gate, then looked at the motley crew behind me.

"Whispers only. No running," I said sternly. I eyed Dilly, who swished her tail and whined low in her throat. "That goes for you too."

The small yard was mostly taken up by a neat wooden shed with several cages inside. The brick walkway to the kitchen door was lined with herbs for cooking. Mrs. Weatherburn had remarked once that Dr. Snow was a vegetarian. This made the doctor all the more special: I'd never known a vegetarian before.

"They can't get out, can they?" Annie said uncertainly, biting the end of a strand of hair.

"It's quite safe, Annie. Dr. Snow built the shed and all the cages himself," I assured her. "He designed the shed so that it has good air, even in summer. See how those sides come down to make these openings? In winter, the sides latch up to protect the animals from the cold."

Bernie and Betsy peered into one of the cages, their eyes round with amazement. "Look, a real bunny," Betsy breathed. "Will it bite?"

I shook my head. "Naw, she's gentle as a kitten."

Betsy stuck her finger through an opening in the wire-mesh cage and wiggled it at a small brown rabbit. She giggled. "She's nibbling my finger. Come pet 'er, Bernie."

"You were right, Florrie. It was good to bring them," I admitted. "Still friends?"

Florrie nodded. "And remember, you can trust your friends. Even with your secrets."

Bernie was soon scampering from one cage to another. "Are these all his pets? Even the mice and guinea pigs?"

"They ain't exactly pets," I told him, putting some clean sheets of newspaper in the mouse cage. "Dr. Snow uses them for experiments."

"What sort of experiments?" Florrie asked. I could tell she didn't want me to launch into gory details of dissected legs and tails.

"Dr. Snow just puts them to sleep, that's all," I explained. "Not permanent-like. Just for a bit."

Betsy frowned. "But why?"

"Dr. Snow's experimenting with a gas called chloroform," I told them. "When you breathe it in, you fall into a kind of sleep—such a deep sleep you don't feel pain. That way, a dentist can yank a nasty tooth out, or a surgeon can cut into you, but you won't feel a thing."

"I don't want to be cut into!" Bernie exclaimed.

"Dr. Snow's been helping dentists and other doctors all over London," I said proudly. "He even gave chloroform to the queen."

"*She* had the toothache?" Annie Ribbons asked, surprised, as though kings and queens should be above that sort of thing.

"No. It was for something else," I explained. "Last year Prince Leopold was born. Dr. Snow helped the queen have her baby prince without feeling much pain."

"Let me see if I understand this," said Florrie slowly. "Dr. Snow tries out the chloroform gas on the creatures first, so he knows how much to give people. I mean, he'd have to, wouldn't 'e? If he made a mistake and gave the queen too much chloroform, they'd have 'is head!"

I nodded. "Exactly. But Dr. Snow is always careful how he treats the animals."

I remembered the day Dr. Snow had appeared. He'd nodded his approval of the clean cages and told me, "We must treat all creatures kindly, and be humane when doing experiments for the betterment of humanity, Eel."

"To think we're standing in the yard of a man who has

actually met the queen, " said Florrie, seeming impressed at last.

"Here's how I know he is truly devoted to science," I said. "Mrs. Weatherburn told me he doesn't just experiment on animals first. He tries out the chloroform on his own self too. He looks at his watch, breathes in the gas, and goes to sleep. Conk!"

I demonstrated, closing my eyes and cocking my head to one side. "Then, when he wakes up after a few minutes, he notes the time in his book and how much chloroform he took. It's all part of bein' a great scientist."

What with Annie Ribbons, Bernie, and Betsy all wanting to help fill the water dishes, feeding took a long time. Finally we were done. Florrie had hung back, and then I saw that she'd been busy drawing.

"One picture for each of you," she told the little ones, tearing out pages from her sketchbook. "Bunnies for Annie and Betsy, and a guinea pig for Bernie."

"Look, Eel," Bernie said, holding it up for me to see. "I'm going to call him General. General the Guinea Pig. Can that be his name from now on?"

"I will call him nothing else," I assured Bernie. "But now it's time for you to go home. Florrie, can you take them?"

"By myself? But I thought we were getting them ices. What about you?"

"I have to talk to Dr. Snow, remember? Please, Florrie," I pleaded.

Florrie sighed. "All right. But what will you do if he's not home? Can you go back to the Lion tonight?"

I shook my head. "If I don't get Dr. Snow's help, I can't. Stealing is serious, you know that."

"What will you do tonight, then? Will you stay here?"

I could feel my face getting red. How did that girl manage to be one step ahead of me at every turn? For it *had* crossed my mind to sleep here. I went over to where Dilly was dozing in the shade and leaned down to scratch her ears, avoiding Florrie's eyes.

"I know you think the world of Dr. Snow, Eel. But swells like him don't care for mudlarks in their backyards," Florrie cautioned. "I'd bet a halfpenny that if Dr. Snow or his housekeeper found you sleeping in this shed, they'd boot you out and tell you not to come back ever again."

If Florrie was right, that would mean losing the only job I still had except mudlarking, which didn't count for much. "Don't worry," I assured her. "I have a place to go."

"Is it safe?"

I nodded. Well, it had been safe enough. But now I wondered: if I slept in one of my old haunts by the Thames, did I risk getting caught by Fisheye Bill?

I reached into my pocket and gave Florrie a sixpence. My last. "Have an ice yourself too."

She sighed. "You'll be missing the best part: holding on to their sticky little hands."

I grinned and waved as they trudged away. Dilly sniffed at every bush, memorizing the yard in case she might want to return someday.

At the gate, Florrie stopped and looked back. "Good luck, Eel."

I was going to need it. I stood staring at the back door, trying to get my courage up. At last I knocked. After what seemed a long time, the door opened. "Hullo, Mrs. Weatherburn," I said, grabbing my cap off my head.

Mrs. Weatherburn was about Dr. Snow's age, which I guessed was around forty. She put me in mind of a bulldog, with a stern face and unsmiling eyes. She was as loyal to the doctor as Dilly was to Mr. Griggs.

To hear Mrs. Weatherburn tell it, she might be working for Prince Albert himself. "Dr. Snow is a genius," she told me every week when I presented myself to get paid. "It's a true privilege to work for him."

"Yes, ma'am, I think so too," I always said.

While I shifted from one foot to the other, Mrs. Weatherburn would go on about how busy the doctor was, how he needed to take better care of his health, and how sure she was that his name would go down in history. Eventually she would stop, give herself a little shake as if recollecting where she was, and, at long last, hand over my two shillings.

Now she looked down at me. "Is there a problem, boy?"

Mrs. Weatherburn never used my name. "I am certainly

not about to call a boy a fish," she had sniffed the first day we'd met.

"No problem at all, Mrs. Weatherburn," I told her. "Everything is done." I stared at my feet. I had to talk fast. "I was wondering, though. Is . . . is Dr. Snow in?"

Mrs. Weatherburn didn't exactly growl; she was far too polite for that. "Before tea? You think you're going to be able to see the doctor at this time of day?"

She didn't wait for an answer. "The doctor is a great man, as you know. And that means he is busy. *Extremely* busy. Most nights he doesn't get home until after dark."

"Yes, ma'am," I put in. "It's just that—"

"Today I believe he's giving chloroform for a tooth extraction." I opened my mouth, but she had already begun speaking again. "They all call upon him now, you know. The best dentists and surgeons in London rely on Dr. Snow. His reputation grows every day. He is a true genius."

Mrs. Weatherburn, I realized suddenly, was right. Dr. Snow was a busy, important man. What had I been thinking? I couldn't expect him to take time to help me. Queen Victoria had been his patient. Why should he care about a mudlark?

"Uh . . . uh, I just wanted to tell you that the cages are all done," I mumbled. "And, um . . . it's Thursday, ma'am." Mrs. Weatherburn usually paid me Thursday evening or Friday morning.

"Ah, so that's it. You want to get paid." She drew two

shillings from her pocket and held them out to me. "He's generous too, boy. Two shillings a week for cleaning cages. You're lucky he took a fancy to you in the market that day."

"Yes, ma'am," I said, taking the coins, which felt cool and solid in my hand.

Two shillings. It was good, but not enough. Not enough to keep my secret safe.

CHAPTER SEVEN
On the River

"Watch it, lad," barked a cabbie.

I leaped aside over a pile of dung, taking care that my two shillings were stuffed deep in my pocket. The cabbie's horse neighed and pawed the cobblestones, shaking its great head at me.

"Best not to get in old General's way," the cabbie warned. I kept my head down and didn't answer. I thought of Bernie, who'd given the tiny guinea pig that same name.

Already Broad Street seemed far away. I was headed for the river, and my old life as a mudlark. I pulled my brown cap down so low its rim rubbed my eyebrows. I walked fast, feeling the bumpy cobblestones through my thin shoes. The bridge was probably two miles away, longer if I kept to the back lanes and alleyways. But that was safer. Pickpockets were sure to be on the prowl in busy places like Piccadilly Circus or Covent Garden.

It wasn't just losing my money that worried me. Almost every pickpocket in London knew Fisheye Bill. Some of his cronies might well recognize me; others would be on the lookout for a boy of my description. All of them would be glad to turn me over to Fisheye for a few shillings.

They weren't the only ones either. Fisheye Bill still had fishmonger pals from the old days, before he took to crime. They often gathered at the open windows of pubs after work, cradling their pints and keeping a sharp eye on everything that went on around them.

I could just imagine one telling my stepfather: "Bill, my friend! I saw that lad of yours today, walkin' right through the market, bold as brass. Run off, has 'e? Now, that's a shame, after all you done for him. His name is Eel, ain't it? Too slippery for you, is 'e?"

Talk like that would make Fisheye Bill boil with rage. He couldn't stomach the fact that I'd been smart enough to disappear. Could I let Fisheye get near me again? *Never.*

The smell of onions and frying potatoes wafting out from the pubs made my stomach growl. I was pinched with hunger, and hadn't touched a morsel since breakfast at the Lion. The Lion. I wondered about Queenie. I wouldn't be there to feed her anymore. How would she get on? Would anyone remember to give her scraps or fill her tin water cup?

Then I thought of Abel Cooper. When the foreman had come in on Monday, he'd found the scrawny black kitten, still a bit damp, curled up in the center of his chair like she owned it. "And who, may I ask, is this?" he'd grumbled.

"This here is Queenie, sir. Some boy threw her into the Thames. Lucky for her I was there," I told him.

"Very gallant of you, I'm sure," Mr. Cooper said sarcastically. "But how did she end up on my chair?"

"Aw, c'mon, Guv, have a heart. Besides, the Lion needs a good ratter."

Abel Cooper grunted. Later, though, when I'd gone back into his office to deliver a message, I found Queenie still on his chair—only this time on his lap.

Queenie would be just fine.

The closer I got to the Thames, the worse the air smelled. I thought about how this day had begun, with Abel Cooper warning of the trouble miasma would bring. As bad as my own troubles were, things were a lot worse for Mr. Griggs. How was he doing now? Maybe I'd been wrong about the blue death. Tomorrow I'd go back and check.

But I had somewhere else to go first thing in the morning. I swallowed hard, thinking about what would happen when I appeared without four shillings. I'd had those shillings yesterday, put away safe in my tin box. But that was yesterday.

I couldn't think of that now. I might not be able to add more than a penny or two to what Mrs. Weatherburn had given me, but I had to try. I had to be a mudlark again, like it or not.

The sour, rotting, filthy smell hit me full in the face as the river came into view. My stomach lurched. Probably just as well it was empty—and likely to stay that way for another day. But luck was on my side—it was low tide.

Pa had taken me for walks by the Thames, I remembered that much. I'm not sure it smelled as bad back then. What I do keep from that time is the feel of his large, firm hand around mine.

Pa never tired of watching the river. "Just look—the barges, the fishing boats, the coming and going of goods!" he'd say, throwing out his arms. "The Thames is like a rich, throbbing blood vessel keeping all of London alive."

Pa felt so sorry for young mudlarks that he sometimes called the littlest ones over to give them a penny. He couldn't have imagined how true his words would turn out to be for me: this river had kept me alive many a day before I got my place at the Lion. And now it would do so again.

I wouldn't get many pennies a day selling coal, bits of wood, or globs of fat tossed overboard by a ship's cook. But it would keep me going. With what I earned from Dr. Snow, I might just be able to make it—at least until winter set in.

With a sudden, fierce stab, I missed Pa. He'd been gone three years now. Just as London was divided by the Thames, my life was divided in two. There was the part before Pa died. Then there was everything else that had come after. More and more, that earlier time seemed to be fading, like a dream that drifts away when you open your eyes to the light.

One moment I was staring at the glittering river. The next I was rammed hard in the back. I went flying through the air and tumbled into the mud. I managed to land on my hands and knees. I leaped up, ready to fight.

"Don't even try, you pigeon." Nasty Ned stood a head taller than me. I cursed myself for being careless. Ned was bad enough. What if it had been Fisheye who'd snuck up behind me?

I wrinkled my nose and stepped back. It was as if Ned took baths in a cesspool. Well, seeing as he was rarely out of the river, that was more or less the case. He narrowed his eyes. "Now, Eel, something's puzzling me."

I brushed mud off my pants, scowling. "I imagine with your tiny brain there's a lot that baffles you."

"I'm just wondering what you're doin' here," he went on, ignoring my insult. "By my count, that's twice this week. I don't mind an occasional morning now and again, given that we're old pals. But here you are back again." He glowered at me, then tipped his river stick under my chin.

I pushed it away. "You don't own the river, Ned."

"Really? I wouldn't be so sure."

He jerked his head to where a few younger boys were wading along the river's edge. "See them lads? They work for me. They're under my protection, so to speak. And I don't like for 'em to come up empty-handed after a day's trolling. I don't like people pushin' in."

"Oh, come on, Ned," I said lightly. "You know I'm a better mudlark than that ragged lot. How about we go in together? It won't be long before you'd be working for me, I wager."

Ned uttered a hoarse growl and swung his stick, this time aiming for my middle. I jumped aside just in time, and barely missed getting prodded in the stomach. Then I ran.

I made for Blackfriars Bridge. Nasty Ned might not want me in his gang, but Thumbless Jake had to put up with me. For all his bluster, he simply didn't move as fast.

By midnight I'd scavenged enough coal to add a penny to my pocket. It was enough for some shrimps or a piece of bread with butter. My belly would have to stay empty, though. I owed this penny elsewhere. I found a place to curl up under the bridge. But I couldn't let myself drop into a deep sleep, not with coins in my pocket. The chances of waking up to find them gone were too great.

As it turned out, I couldn't have slept even if I'd wanted

to; my mind was as choppy as the river in a strong wind. I kept seeing Hugzie's smug smile, Betsy and Bernie sitting so still and scared, Mr. Griggs writhing in pain.

I tossed and turned on the hard stone. I'd have to get used to it. I'd been a mudlark before. I could do it again. I was good at it. That's what made Thumbless Jake first notice me.

"Hey, you, lad. Get over here," he'd called out one evening when the fog had shrouded everything in strange, blurry shadows. It was dangerous when it got like that. A barge or other boat could come upon you so sudden there was barely time to move out of the way in the thick, sludgy water.

"I been watchin' you," Thumbless Jake declared. "You make a good haul. If I didn't know better, I'd say you could peer through the murk. You been a mudlark long?"

I shrugged. "Not long."

"Hmph. Well, I don't know how you're doin' so well, but keep your distance," he warned, raising his stump of a thumb in my face. "I might be missing this, but I still got another hand that can wring a boy's neck if 'e gets in my way."

CHAPTER EIGHT
In Which I Visit
Mrs. Miggle's Lodging House

Friday, September 1

First thing I did the next morning was check my pocket. All safe.

I sold the rope and the few copper nails I'd managed to find to a rag shop for a penny. Then I was on my way— me and everyone else. Our feet tapped out the rhythms of a new day: the slap of bare feet on cobblestones, the clomp of hard leather boots, the brisk click of ladies' heels. It seemed a wonder that the cobblestones weren't worn down flat.

By the time I reached a little warren of streets near Field Lane, it was seven. The streets were already shimmering with heat. I slipped round to the back of a small house and knocked softly at the kitchen door.

"So it's you." A large, red-faced woman opened the door a crack and peered at me. "Got it?"

"Mrs. Miggle, I do," I whispered, looking over my shoulder. I shifted from one foot to the other and fished inside my pocket. I wanted her to invite me in—now. The smell of warm, fresh biscuits and coffee enveloped me, sending an actual pain through my stomach. I was that hungry.

She held the door open and I slid in. Now was the time to say it.

"Leastwise, I have half," I said, holding out the money.

Mrs. Miggle snapped it up, quick as a frog snatching a bug. Before I knew it, the shillings had disappeared into some hidden place in her vast skirts. I reached into my other pocket and drew out the penny I'd gotten that morning. "And here's payment for the ragged school."

Mrs. Miggle took that too, then folded her arms across her wide body and glared down at me. "So where's the rest? Where's the other two shillings?"

I wondered if she had *ever* smiled. Mrs. Miggle couldn't be more than thirty, yet she seemed as stern and hard as if she'd had all the softness rubbed away years before.

"I've been easy with you, young man, on account of I have such a big heart, but I have much to bear." She leaned so close I could see tiny hairs sticking out of her upper lip. "Much."

"Yes, ma'am. I do realize that, and I am grateful for your kindnesses," I said quickly. "And if, just this once, you could give me until next Friday, I swear I'll have the four shillings for next week, and the two I still owe for this. Plus a penny for the Field Lane Ragged School fee."

I cast my head down, forced a tear out of one eye, and did my best to look forlorn. It sometimes worked, even for someone as hard-hearted as the formidable Mrs. Miggle.

"All right. No need to pull that pathetic act on me." Mrs. Miggle couldn't be fooled. She turned away to take the kettle off the stove.

"How is he, ma'am?"

"'E's just fine," she said shortly, measuring out some tea. "Goin' to the ragged school every day, like we agreed. But 'e grows, you know.

"Boys have an awful habit of doing that, whether you want them to or not," she went on in a complaining whine. Mrs. Miggle had a high voice, like a fiddle that wasn't tuned. "I can't be expected to get 'im new shoes and clothes. Not on what you pay for 'is keep. I got real lodgers to worry about."

"I know, Mrs. Miggle. I'm working on getting more money for the winter," I assured her. "I'll get him a new pair of shoes, and a coat too. But there's time yet."

I paused, wondering how to put what I wanted to say next. "Mrs. Miggle," I began. "You haven't . . . you haven't seen anything out of the ordinary of late?"

She narrowed her eyes. "Like what?"

I licked my lip and tried to sound casual. "Oh, just someone nosin' around, maybe one of my old mudlark pals."

63

"You're not in trouble for thievin', are you, boy?"

"No, 'course not," I said quickly. "It's no matter. Can I . . . can I talk to him?"

She went to a back room off the kitchen, no larger than a cupboard. I followed, peering in past her at the small sleeping boy.

"Henry, lad," called Mrs. Miggle. "Your big brother's here to see you."

"Henry," I said softly. "Wake up. It's me."

I went to sit on the edge of the narrow straw mattress. Henry startled upright, a hint of fear in his face until he realized it was me.

"Eel! Did you come to take me away?" he whispered, his dark eyes darting toward the kitchen. "Mrs. Miggle . . . she's mean."

I frowned. "As mean as *him*?"

"Nothin' like that." He rubbed sleep from his eyes. "Just a bit rough."

"Mrs. Miggle is an honest woman," I told him.

Though even as I said it, I wondered: was she? For now, she was content with the four shillings a week I paid for Henry's room and board. But if Fisheye found out where Henry was, would Mrs. Miggle be happy to hand him over for one large sum?

A lad like Henry was worth a lot to Fisheye. Henry

could be made to steal and run simple cons. With his sweet face and high voice, he could bring in money by begging, especially if he was taught to cry. I couldn't let Fisheye find my little brother, no matter what.

Henry dressed and went to sit on a low stool in the kitchen, where Mrs. Miggle gave him bread dipped in bacon grease and a cup of milk. She must've been feeling more kindly toward me than she let on, because I got some bread too.

"It's just the crust," she said, not willing to admit she had a soft heart somewhere inside.

Henry didn't want me to leave. "Will you walk me to school, Eel?"

"Not today," I told him as Mrs. Miggle gave me a cup of water (her generosity did not extend as far as milk). I couldn't take the chance of our being spotted together.

"My time's up anyway. I've got to go now, Henry." I finished gulping down the cool water and patted the top of his head.

"Wait!" Jumping up, he scrambled back into his little cupboard of a room and came back with a slip of paper, folded once and crumpled.

He grinned, which made his dark eyes sparkle like coal in sunlight. "Go on, Eel. Open it."

I read it out loud while my little brother sat and giggled beside me.

September 1, 1854

To my brother Eel,
Manny hapy returns of the day.
                    Ever your loving brother,
                                Henry

I gave him a hug. I was glad to see that his bones weren't sticking out the way they had last winter. Mrs. Miggle might seem rough, but she wouldn't let him starve. "You keep at your writing, Henry. Mum would be proud."

I left soon after, tucking the note into my pocket and patting it as I walked away. It was like a promise for comfort later, I thought, almost like having a small meat pie wrapped in paper waiting at the end of a long day.

I'd forgotten about my birthday. It was about to be the worst one anyone could imagine.

PART TWO

The Blue Death

The most terrible outbreak of cholera which ever occurred in this kingdom, is probably that which took place in Broad Street, Golden Square.

—Dr. John Snow,
On the Mode of Communication of Cholera (1855)

The people stood by one another, in this season of peril and perplexity, with unflinching and admirable courage.

—Rev. Henry Whitehead,
The Cholera in Berwick Street (1854)

CHAPTER NINE
The First Coffin

Later that morning, I was back on Broad Street, looking up at Mr. Griggs's window. I'd already walked miles. I rubbed a crick in my neck. I felt stiff from spending the night outside. *No use complaining,* I reminded myself.

I was still a bit hungry, even though Mrs. Miggle, in honor of my special day, had given me two fresh biscuits to stick in my pockets when I left. I'd stopped at the Warwick Street pump to wash the rest of the mud off my legs. I'd doused my head too and had a good drink of water.

I was about to go upstairs to see Mr. Griggs when Dilly came trotting around the corner and rushed right at me, putting her paws up on my chest and whining softly.

"Where have you come from, then?" I asked, scratching the soft spot behind her silky ears.

I looked up, half expecting to see Mr. Griggs himself strolling down Broad Street. Dilly often tagged along with him when he made deliveries to his best customers.

There was no Mr. Griggs in sight. What would happen to the dog—to the whole family—if he didn't recover? Mrs. Griggs wouldn't be able to keep the shop, I knew that. Things would be hard. I thought of what Mum had told Henry and me after Pa died: "It's no small thing to lose a father. The world is a cruel place for fatherless children."

But even she had no idea how cruel. I thought Mr. Dickens had named his last book well: *Hard Times*. In front of me the tailor shop was closed and dark. No sounds came from the room above. I should go in, I knew. Instead I stood there, talking nonsense to a dog.

"Well, if I still had my situation at the Lion, I'd take you with me on an errand this fine day," I told her. "But my destination is right here—to check on your master, Mr. Griggs."

Still, I didn't move. I stood squinting in the thick, oily sunlight. I wiped sweat from my forehead. *I don't want to go in there,* I thought suddenly. *I can't do it.*

"Eel!" It was Florrie. She and Betsy hurried toward me, with the Reverend Henry Whitehead behind them. Everyone who lived near the Golden Square knew the young assistant curate at St. Luke's. The reverend was a tall man, bright and curious as a robin.

When we'd first met and he'd asked if I could read, he'd

told me, "Schooling is important. I was lucky in that regard, lad. I grew up by the seaside, in a town called Ramsgate. My father was headmaster of Chatham House, and I was able to attend because I was his son. It was a better school than we could have ever afforded. That's how I got the chance to go to Oxford."

I thought it strange that such an educated man would bother to talk to me. But that was Rev. Whitehead. He knew everyone in the neighborhood, and greeted young and old with the same friendly smile, whether they turned up in St. Luke's for Sunday service or not. (And mostly, I did not.)

My heart sank as I looked at his grim face. It wasn't hard to guess that Mrs. Griggs had sent for him. The reverend said softly, "I'm afraid we have a sad errand at Betsy's house."

"I was here yesterday afternoon and looked in on Mr. Griggs then," I said. "Has there been a change?"

"Why don't you come along, Eel?" he suggested, not answering me directly. "You and Florrie can stay in the shop with the children while I have a word with their mother."

Then he leaned over and put a hand on my shoulder. His voice was low but calm. "I fear the worst."

Despite the heat, a shiver ran over my skin.

"I want to see my pa," Betsy piped up. "Don't make me stay downstairs in the shop. I don't like it there without Pa."

Florrie and I glanced at Rev. Whitehead, who nodded. "It may bring him comfort."

At the top of the stairs, the reverend knocked and

pushed the door open. At first everything appeared to be much the same as the day before. Then I looked closer and swallowed, trying to keep from crying out or, worse, losing the breakfast Mrs. Miggle had given me.

It was hard to tell that Mr. Griggs was alive. His eyes had shrunk in his face, which now seemed as pinched and dried as that of an elderly man. His poor body was no more than an old gray rag that had been wrung out to dry, or the light, papery carcass of a bird left to crackle in the sun.

Worst of all, his lips were a dark blue. Suddenly I understood. *This is why they call cholera "the blue death."* He'd lost so much liquid from the inside that his skin and lips were no longer pink and healthy, but blue and dried out.

Mrs. Griggs turned to nod at Rev. Whitehead, then put her fingers gently on her husband's wrist. The reverend stepped forward and knelt beside Mr. Griggs. Bernie lay huddled in the corner, sucking his thumb, his eyes wide. He looked too scared to cry.

"Come and say your goodbye now, Betsy," Mrs. Griggs said softly.

Betsy hung back, her bony shoulders quivering under her thin dress. Beside me, Florrie had started to shiver too, even though the room was stifling hot.

"Take my hand, Betsy," I whispered. *I know exactly what this is like,* I thought.

"Go ahead, dear girl," Rev. Whitehead encouraged her. "Kiss your father's forehead and whisper in his ear. He can still hear your voice."

I watched Betsy put her small hand on her father's shoulder, careful-like, as if she were afraid to cause him more pain. She was a brave girl, Betsy. Her hand didn't tremble.

But if Mr. Griggs did catch his daughter's whisper, it was the last sound he heard.

We stood without saying anything for a long time. I can't exactly explain it, but I remembered feeling this way before, when my father died. It was as if the moment was bigger than any of us. It was like Death had tiptoed in among us, freezing us in our places until he'd done his work and left. And what Death did was solemn and awful.

I remember my mother telling Henry and me, "Don't worry about touching your pa. He can't feel any pain now."

Not long after, two men with bored, blank faces had come knocking at our door. I remembered those men, stumbling up the stairs, making jokes about dropping the corpse. They had stopped talking when they reached the top. For I was there, standing at the open door, waiting and watching them.

"Sorry, lad," one whispered as I stepped aside to let them go by.

Bernie began to cry. He ran to his mum, who let out a hoarse, exhausted sob. Rev. Whitehead pulled the sheet over the tailor's face. He nodded to Florrie and me. "Maybe the little ones would like a bit of air while I speak with their mum."

Florrie got Bernie to his feet. I took Betsy's hand again. "Dilly's downstairs. We'd better go see her before she gets into some sort of trouble."

Outside, I found a piece of rope and threw it for Dilly to chase. Betsy and Bernie watched, looking dazed.

Annie Lewis came down to fill a bucket at the Broad Street pump. She stared at Betsy and Bernie, then came to me and tugged on my shirt. "Is Mr. Griggs dead, Eel? My mum told me he was awful sick."

"Yes, Annie Ribbons, I'm afraid so. Can you come and be with Betsy later? I'm sure she'd like to have you near."

Annie bit her lip and shook her head. "Mum needs me." Then she went back inside without another word.

After a while Rev. Whitehead came out, rubbing a clean white handkerchief across his forehead. "Take Bernie to your mother now, Betsy," he told her gently. "She'll find your company a comfort."

He looked up and down Broad Street and sighed deeply. From where we stood we could see people going in and out of shops, or heading to the pump with buckets to fill. A man called out in a cheerful voice, "Good day to you, Reverend Whitehead. Have you ever seen anything to beat the likes of this heat?"

The reverend answered him pleasantly. But when the man had gone, he turned to us. "Ah, children, it breaks my heart to see this bustling street now. Before long it will be full of nothing but coffin carts."

"It's truly the blue death?" I asked, though I already knew the answer.

"Yes. The symptoms leave no doubt of it."

"Maybe Mr. Griggs will be the only one," Florrie said hopefully.

"I'm afraid not, my dear." Rev. Whitehead shook his head. "I've already received word that others were taken ill last night."

"Can anything be done to keep it from spreading?" Florrie asked, twirling one braid about her finger. It was what she did when she was nervous.

"Well, men will pour lime to try to clean the infection from the streets," Rev. Whitehead told us. "But as for the poison in the air that causes the cholera, there is little people can do except flee this polluted place.

"And now I must be off to visit other families," he added. "Take care of yourselves."

He squared his shoulders and strode away, like a soldier going into battle.

"What do you think will happen now?" Florrie asked.

"I don't know," I admitted.

But then, right before our eyes, the street began to change. A woman rushed past, a pillowcase stuffed with belongings bouncing against her back. A little boy trotted behind her, sobbing, trying to keep up. A man carrying a screaming toddler burst out of a nearby house and almost ran into us. Florrie and I jumped back out of his way.

"I guess Reverend Whitehead was right," I said. "Families are leaving. And fast."

"What about you, Eel?"

"Me?" I hadn't thought that far. "I don't actually live on Broad Street anymore. But this is my neighborhood. My friends are here—well, at least you are. I'm staying. Maybe I can help. Besides, I don't have anywhere else to go."

A man came by and hung a yellow flag on a post on Berwick Street.

It's a warning for people to stay away, I realized. A warning that the Great Trouble was upon us all.

CHAPTER TEN
The Coffin Men

A little while later, we saw the first coffin cart rolling toward us. It had come for Mr. Griggs.

Betsy and Bernie were with their mother. Dilly lay inside the shop, curled up in the shadows, almost as if she were waiting for Mr. Griggs to appear and take up his scissors and needle again. When she heard the horse and cart, she rushed to the doorway to bark at the men.

"Quiet, girl," I ordered.

"Hold my horse's head, will you, laddie?" asked one of the men, who had orange hair so like Nasty Ned's I wondered if they were related. He was so cheerful it was hard to think of him as a coffin man.

The men lifted a wooden coffin out of the back of the

cart. They carried it past us, and we could hear them struggling to get it up the stairs. They came stumbling back down a few minutes later. A shiver went through me as I watched them load the long box into the cart. You could tell it was heavier now.

"Poor Mr. Griggs," Florrie said, tears filling her eyes. "He was the first, I guess."

The man with the orange hair overheard her.

"This poor man might've been the first, but it won't be long before we're cartin' folks off by the tens. We're headed over to Peter Street now." He climbed into the cart and took up the reins. "Word is that whole families were struck sick last night."

"Might be hundreds before it's over," the other man remarked, scrambling up beside him. "Nasty business, especially in this heat. I'll be sweatin' like a—"

At that moment a girl came rushing toward us, waving her hands. "Wait!"

"What is it, lass?" asked the friendly driver.

"Come and take them away, will you, sir?" she begged, breathing hard. "My mum's gone. My big sister too. Please, sir. Please come."

I wondered how many people had been watching the coffin men from their windows. Even before the cart had turned the corner, more houses began to empty out. The cobblestones rang with the trampling feet of wild-eyed mothers and fathers, hauling toddlers by the hand, with bulging pillowcases of clothes tossed over their backs.

"But where can they go?" said Florrie, stepping back into the tailor's doorway so as not to get hit by a woman with a basket of bedding on her hip.

"Anywhere away from here." I shrugged. "Maybe they have relatives or friends somewhere else in London, or even the countryside."

"I'm not afraid to stay," Florrie declared. "Are you, Eel?"

"Not me. I'm strong." I tried to sound confident.

But Florrie's face had gone white and she tapped her foot nervously. "I'd better head home, though. Mum will be worried."

I watched her run off, her braids bumping against the thin fabric of her dress. "Florrie!"

She stopped and looked back at me.

"You be careful now, Florrie Baker," I called. I wasn't sure how to put the feeling I had into words. "Be careful, on account . . ."

My face turned red. Florrie grinned. "On account of we're friends, silly."

As she ran off, I said to myself, "Be careful 'cause you're grand, Florrie Baker." *The grandest girl I know.*

✻ ✻ ✻

I stood alone, a small knot of fear in my stomach. No one was safe from the cholera. Not Florrie or the Griggses or the Lewises or Rev. Whitehead. Or me.

I wasn't scared so much for myself. But if I got sick, what would happen to Henry?

But how did you stop the cholera from getting you? If it was poison in the air like everyone said, there was nothing I could do. We all had to breathe. And I'd been breathin' the same air as Mr. Griggs.

It must be a matter of luck, then. Or something else. I had no idea. And looking at the folks streaming past me, I didn't think anyone else did either.

A few minutes later, a man down the road waved to get my attention. "Here, boy! I'll give you a penny if you help me load this cart I borrowed to take my family out of here."

I sprinted over, glad of the money. Next Friday would come soon enough, and Mrs. Miggle would expect to be paid the four shillings I owed her, plus the two I'd been short this week.

As it turned out, that penny was just the beginning. There was tin to be had from the panic that struck Broad Street that Friday, and though I didn't like profiting from misfortune, I was grateful to hear the chink of coins in my pocket.

All that afternoon I ran up and down Broad Street and

the smaller lanes surrounding it—Dufours Place, Cambridge Street, and Hopkins Street. I went down Poland, Berwick, Marshall, and Cross Streets. Everywhere it was the same: frightened families rushing to escape the blue death.

Sometimes I got a penny or two for helping to load a cart. Other times a harried mother asked me to carry a basket down a steep flight of steps. The streets were crowded with people, scurrying in all directions. There were more coffin carts too.

It was nearly dark before I made my way down Regent Street to Dr. Snow's neighborhood. Sackville Street felt like another world: quiet and peaceful, with just a few gentlemen and ladies out for an evening stroll. *They don't even know what's happening less than a mile away,* I thought.

I was so tired after feeding the animals I almost curled up in a corner of the shed. But I didn't dare risk Mrs. Weatherburn catching me. I'd best go back to the river. I might even be able to troll for coal before going to sleep. The tide was low, perfect for mudlarking. A half-moon would be up soon; the moon grew rounder and brighter every night.

I made my way to Blackfriars Bridge, stopping just once to buy a loaf of bread and the end of a round of cheese. I spotted Thumbless Jake in the distance, his tall shape almost fuzzy in the strange yellowy light. I kept out of his way. I didn't want Jake being tempted to turn me in to Fisheye.

I found a stretch of river I could work in peace. Most of the regulars had stopped to get bread and a pint of beer with their day's earnings. Or maybe the stench had gotten too much.

The moon cast a glittery light on the water as I waded through the thick slime, my eyes on the shallows and the edge of the bank. The weather might be warm, but folks still needed coal for cooking. I wouldn't ignore iron, copper, or even bits of wood, but coal was my first choice. I looked for lumps dropped by bargemen as they heaved their loads to the shore.

After a while I found an empty barge tied up near some of the old tumbledown wooden factories that hugged the river's edge. I scrambled up a rope and wedged myself between two rows of barrels on the deck. It would have to do.

It was a little more comfortable than the night before, and I was tired enough. But I couldn't get to sleep. My mind raced from one trouble to another: the blue death and what it meant for folks on Broad Street; Mr. Griggs and the way he'd looked, all blue and dried out; Fisheye Bill; and what the future might hold for Henry and me.

I'd begun to have hope when I was at the Lion. I was proud of my work and had learned a lot. Sometimes I'd even had the courage to make a suggestion to Abel Cooper. Once, after I'd come up with a system for double-checking the orders we sent out, the foreman had patted my shoulder. "Old Jake was right about you, lad. You may look a bit wild, with those inky black eyes you got, but you notice things. Good work."

Good work. If it hadn't been for Hugzie, I would still be there, with a real job—and, most important, a way to keep Henry safe. My mind ached from too many thoughts, and my stomach ached from not enough food. And then, just before sleep finally took me, I remembered again: today had been my birthday.

CHAPTER ELEVEN
Bernie

Saturday, September 2

"Where is he?"

I came awake instantly. Vaguely I realized that I was stiff, stuffed as I was into the small space between the rows of barrels on the barge. But that didn't matter. What mattered was the voice. I knew that voice.

"Don't deny it, Jake. That weasely little urchin ain't dead," Fisheye Bill Tyler was saying. "My guess is he's been out here mudlarkin'. And that means you seen him."

"Now, Bill, I can't say yes and I can't say no," Jake answered. "All these boys look about the same to me."

"Don't give me that. You know Eel—the scrawny one with eyes like a Tower raven," growled Fisheye. "This is a serious business, Jake. That boy's got something that belongs to me. Somethin' I have a right to. I have a right to him too, if it comes to it."

"I dunno nothin' 'bout it," squeaked Jake. I didn't dare lift up my head. But I could almost see Fisheye squeezing his arm.

"Don't expect me to believe that," Fisheye Bill scoffed. I could imagine his cold glare. Men like Jake didn't fare well under Fisheye's gaze. He went on. "Now, my friend, are you gonna tell me where he's at, or do I have to break off your other thumb?"

"Like I told you before, Bill, I ain't seen Eel for months," came Jake's complaining whine. "I thought the lad was dead." So Jake hadn't been the one to rat on me. At least, not yet.

"Besides, ain't Eel a big lad now? Too old for what you want 'im for?" Jake went on. "That lad's too growed up to slip through windows like a little snakesman so you can break into houses."

"You never mind that," I heard Fisheye Bill say. "That's my business."

"Well, Bill, I got business to attend to meself. So leave me to it, won't you?" Jake said. "Turn your nose up at me if you will, but at least a scavenger's life is honest."

I grinned. Jake was holding his own with Fisheye Bill. His voice faded, and I figured he must be wading through the sludgy water toward Tower Bridge. I crouched lower in my hiding place, fighting the urge to poke my head up and lay my eyes on Fisheye Bill Tyler just to prove this wasn't a nightmare.

"Come on, Jake. What say you and me take a break from this stinking place and head over to a pub?" Fisheye said. "You can rest your legs. I'll even buy you some breakfast and a beer to go with it."

There was a pause. "Or maybe a gin, if you'd rather."

I froze. Jake might not have said anything about me before now. But if Fisheye lured him to his side with the promise of gin, who knew what might happen? Jake could end up telling him how he'd gotten me a nice situation at the Lion Brewery over on Broad Street.

I strained my ears to catch Jake's answer. I might not be at the Lion anymore, but I didn't want Fisheye poking around anywhere near Broad Street. I could only hope that if Jake did talk, that yellow-flag warning of the cholera would keep Fisheye Bill away.

"Another time, Bill. Another time," came Jake's voice at last. I let my breath out. I was still safe.

When I got back to Broad Street that morning, the first person I saw was Rev. Whitehead. He looked as if he hadn't slept.

"Are things worse, sir?" I asked.

"I'm afraid so," he said, wiping his brow with a handkerchief. "I spent most of the night visiting families. Yet there isn't much I can do."

He rubbed a hand over his eyes, and I could see dark circles under them. "It strikes so viciously—so quickly," he went on. "Mrs. Griggs herself is near death and—"

His words sent a jolt through me. "That can't be! She was fine yesterday."

Rev. Whitehead laid a hand on my shoulder. "I'm sorry, Eel. I forgot you didn't know. She became ill last evening. Bernie too."

"Bernie! But . . ." I could hardly believe what I was hearing. "But if Mrs. Griggs is sick, who is helping them? Betsy is too small. She can't—"

He raised a hand. "Calm yourself, lad. Florrie Baker is there, and as capable a nurse as I've ever seen."

"Florrie! But . . . will she get it by being so close to sick people?"

"I fear everyone may be in danger from the filthy air and ill-ventilated rooms of this neighborhood," he replied. "The atmosphere in these crowded streets is unwholesome indeed. Miasma is the cause of this pestilence."

Poor Mrs. Griggs, I thought. She had just watched her husband die. She knew what would almost certainly happen to her. Mrs. Griggs was devoted to her children. It would break her heart to be so sick she couldn't care for Bernie.

Just then I caught sight of Dr. Rogers, about to turn onto Poland Street. He waved at Rev. Whitehead without smiling and shook his head. Annie's mum, Mrs. Lewis, had mentioned that he was the doctor her family relied on. Probably many other families did too. One look at his face told me he was powerless to help against this terrible disease.

No, Dr. Rogers couldn't help. *But what about Dr. Snow?*

It might be a foolish plan. After all, Dr. Snow treated the queen herself. Would he care about the poor people on the other side of Regent Street?

It was worth a try. I'd given up on asking Dr. Snow to help me get my situation back. That was a small thing—just one mudlark who wanted to keep his job.

But this—this was about a whole neighborhood suffering.

And it was about Bernie.

Fifteen minutes later, I'd snaked my way through the crowds on Regent Street and was banging on Dr. Snow's back door. Mrs. Weatherburn opened it, adjusting her cap and looking at me with a keen, stern expression. "Yes, boy? What is it you want now? As you will recollect, I paid you last night."

"Yes, ma'am. Thank you. It's just that I need to see Dr. Snow, please. It's urgent."

She arched her eyebrows in surprise. "Well, that may be, but I'm afraid Dr. Snow left early to attend a surgeon in Kensington."

I felt panic rising inside. "But . . . we need him. The people on Broad Street need him."

She frowned. "For what?"

"He hasn't heard, then?" I asked. "The cholera has hit.

Broad Street and Berwick Street, Poland Street and Little Windmill Street—the whole neighborhood near the Golden Square."

Mrs. Weatherburn stepped back, as if she might catch it just from being near me. I wondered if Dr. Snow would be too frightened to come to Broad Street; even doctors could get deadly diseases. Maybe he would think the air in our neighborhood was too dangerous.

"I don't believe he has heard about the outbreak," she said. "He's been so busy I've barely seen him myself."

"I'd like to at least tell him about it. Will he be back soon?"

"Not until after dark."

I stared up at her for a minute, then turned and walked away. I kicked a stone on the path, swallowing hard, feeling tears sting my eyes. Mr. Griggs had barely lasted a day. How long could Bernie fight the blue death?

"Have you given the cages a thorough cleaning lately, boy?" Mrs. Weatherburn called after me. "I've noticed quite a pungent smell the last day or two. It's not enough just to feed them, you know. It's probably time to change all the bedding."

"Yes, ma'am," I replied. You couldn't put anything over on Mrs. Weatherburn.

All I could think of as I cleaned the cages was how much Betsy and Bernie had liked petting the bunnies. I wanted everything to go back to the way it had been two days ago.

"It ain't fair," I said. "It just ain't fair."

* * *

Since Dr. Snow wouldn't be home for hours, I headed back to Broad Street. Even though most families had escaped, I might still have a chance to make some money. And I did— though not at all in the way I expected.

The first person I ran into was the cheerful-looking driver with the bright orange hair. "Hey there. Aren't you the lad I saw yesterday?" he called out. "My mate's taken off. Weak stomach. Want to earn a few pence?"

"Yes, sir." I couldn't forget Henry. "What . . . what do you want me to do?"

"Whaddya think? Just help me load bodies into coffins, and coffins into the cart," he explained, wiping his sweaty face with a ragged handkerchief. He glanced at me. "Don't worry, son. I'll wrap them in a clean cloth first."

I swallowed hard. *Lift a coffin? Touch a dead body, even through a sheet?*

The man leaned forward and put a large, rough hand on my shoulder. As if reading my mind, he said, "You *can* do it, laddie. These are your neighbors, ain't they?"

Still, I hesitated.

"I'll give you two shillings if you work till sunset," he offered.

"All right," I agreed. "But . . . I might have a weak stomach too."

"Just don't fall down flat in a faint," the man said, pleasant as ever.

I *did* feel sick to my stomach at first. And then I didn't. It wasn't that I got used to it, nothing like that. It was more that, sometime in the first hour of walking into those hot, shadowy rooms where death had been, I found a way to change my thinking around.

Instead of looking with my eyes, I decided to see with my heart. I tried to remember that the corpses were just people. People like Mr. Griggs, or neighbors I might greet on the street.

And so, rather than thinking about my own queasy feelings, I thought about them. I started to believe there was something important and noble about what we were doing. It made me want to be different from the men who'd come to get my own pa. And this coffin man, whose name was Charlie, seemed to feel the same way.

"I don't hold with jokin' around corpses or not bein' respectful to them that's left behind," Charlie had told me early on as we carried a plain wooden coffin into a house. "We'll all be going into the ground one of these days. And it might be sooner than we know."

That coffin was a small one. I swallowed hard. I didn't meet the gaze of the child's mother, who kept hold of her little son's hand, not able to let go.

"You ever lost someone close to you, lad?" Charlie said softly as we loaded the small, plain box into the cart.

"My parents. First my pa. When I was nine." I didn't know why I was telling this to a stranger. "I didn't even know he was sick at first. But he kept coughing and coughing till he got so weak. . . ."

"The consumption." Charlie nodded knowingly. "I had a cousin went that way. How 'bout your mum, then? She gone too?"

"Less than three years after my father. Last September. Just about a year ago now."

"Broken heart, was it?"

I didn't answer. Though that wasn't a bad guess. Not a bad guess at all.

Charlie and I loaded coffins onto the cart all that long, hot day. Once the cart was full, we headed over to the undertaker's to unload and to pick up more empty coffins. Charlie was careful to mark each coffin with the name of the dead person.

"Don't want to get 'em mixed up, though some would say it don't matter," he remarked. "But I don't hold with that. If I go to visit a grave, I want to know that I'm talking to the right person."

The sweat ran down my face. I'm not ashamed to say that it got mixed with tears more than once. The cholera had struck Broad Street hardest of all. But we also went into houses on Poland Street, Hopkins Street, Peter Street, and Berwick Street, where Florrie and her family lived.

It was dusk by the time we stopped. I felt worn out and sick at heart. I barely had strength to move. Charlie gave me two shillings for my work, and said he guessed he had a cousin who'd be able to help him the next day.

I looked at the shillings greedily. I'd already spent the pennies I'd gotten yesterday on a roll and a bit of cheese. I hadn't felt much like eating all day. But now, suddenly, I was ravenous. I imagined biting into a hot meat pie or a piece of bread spread thick with butter.

No, I told myself. *I should save these shillings to give to Mrs. Miggle.*

"You done good," Charlie was saying. "You're such a thin, shadowy lad I feared you might scare the little orphans. But when you smile, you light up, like moonlight. And the kiddies took to you, they did, after all."

He brought out a small basket that had been sitting at his feet in the cart. He opened it and held out a bottle of ginger beer and a large meat pie.

"I can't eat till the end of the day in this job, but then I gets so hungry I can't make it home without a nibble," Charlie admitted with a grin. "My wife packed more than enough. So here—you've earned it, lad."

I'm sure my eyes were as round as saucers by that point. And when I took my first bite of that flaky crust, I didn't think a meal had ever tasted so good.

After Charlie left, I tiptoed up the stairs at 40 Broad Street. As I was about to knock, I looked over at the door to the room Annie Ribbons shared with her parents and baby sister, Fanny. I hadn't seen Annie since yesterday. I wondered if the Lewises had decided to leave, as so many other families had. At least Charlie and I hadn't had to go in there.

Florrie opened the door and stuffed her little sketchbook back into her apron pocket. She stuck her pencil into the top of one braid. "Where have you been? I thought you'd come by earlier."

"I've been helping the coffin man," I said. Then I closed my mouth. That was all I would say. I could never tell Florrie, or Henry, or anyone, what I had seen and heard and done.

Dilly pushed past Florrie and flopped at my feet, grinning the way dogs do. Her tail thumped wildly on the worn wooden floorboards with a loud swishing noise. "Quiet, girl," I said, scratching her ears.

"How . . . how are they?" I whispered.

"I don't know. It's awful scary, Eel. They're sleeping now, even Betsy," Florrie said. "I never seen the cholera before."

"How about your family?"

"For now, everyone's fine. Nancy's out helping neighbors, same as me. Pa's working. Danny brought over some meat pies Mum made." Florrie paused to take a sip of water from a jug. "My mother ain't so good with sickness herself. Just faints away and is no help to anyone."

Mrs. Griggs stirred and moaned.

"I've made up my mind, Florrie. I've decided to ask Dr. Snow to come see Bernie and Mrs. Griggs. He's been out on doctor business all day. But I'm going there tonight," I promised. "And I'll sleep in the shed if he's not there. I won't let him leave in the morning until he hears me out. He'll help them, I know he will."

"Will you still ask him to help you with Mr. Huggins?"

"It's too late," I said, shaking my head. "Mr. Huggins won't believe anything I say now. I can't go back. Besides, this is more important."

"Everything is different now, ain't it?" said Florrie softly. "It's like the whole world changed."

Florrie glanced over at Betsy, who lay curled up a bit apart from her mother and brother. Betsy's cheeks were flushed from the heat. At least she still looked healthy and pink, not blue and pale. Maybe Betsy would be lucky.

Florrie patted the sketchbook in her pocket. "I'm not sure if it was the proper thing to do, but I made some drawings of Bernie and Mrs. Griggs today. If the worst does happen, Betsy will have something to remind her of the way they looked."

"The worst won't happen," I said fiercely. "It can't."

The stillness was suddenly broken by an odd sound. I realized it was coming from me. The meat pie had been so delicious it had made me hungry for more.

"That's your stomach," said Florrie, stifling a smile.

She went to a basket by the wall and took out a slice of bread, spread thick with butter. "Danny brought this too. I can't eat it," she said. "You take it."

"Thanks."

Dilly stared up at me with soft, begging eyes. I broke off a piece, and she snapped it out of the air. Florrie grinned. "No wonder they call you Eel. You're as thin as one."

She gestured to a bucket in the corner. "Want some water?"

I shook my head. "No, thanks. The coffin man just gave me a ginger beer."

"Lucky you. Ginger beer is my favorite," said Florrie. "You could've saved me some."

"Next time," I promised.

I sat with Florrie for a while, then bid her good night and set out. It was dark now. I was extra careful on Regent Street to watch for pickpockets. When I got to Sackville Street, I gave the creatures in Dr. Snow's menagerie more water. The rabbits' eyes glowed in the silvery moonlight.

The lights in Dr. Snow's house were out. It was too late to knock on the door. I'd have to try in the morning. *I should go to the river to sleep,* I thought. But I couldn't move another step. I felt tired from the inside out. I curled up in a corner of the shed and used my cap for a pillow.

The animals rustled and moved restlessly. They weren't used to me being there except to feed them. I tossed and turned too. I squeezed my eyes shut against the pictures that filled my mind, but it didn't help. In the end, I'm not ashamed to say, I cried myself to sleep.

CHAPTER TWELVE
In Dr. Snow's Study

Sunday, September 3

"Yes? May I help you, lad?" A pair of keen brown eyes gazed at me curiously.

Dr. Snow himself!

"Uh . . . uh, yes, sir. . . ." I snatched the cap from my head, which sent a lock of hair spilling into my eyes. I tried to brush it away, which made me drop the cap.

I hadn't expected Dr. Snow to answer the door himself. I'd almost forgotten his strange voice, hoarse and husky. *Maybe this was a bad idea,* I thought as I picked up my cap. *He probably doesn't even remember my name. What makes me think he'll come to help Bernie just because I ask?*

Finally I planted myself before him, cap held respectful-like in my hands as Mum had taught me. "Please, sir . . . I need . . ."

The words stuck in my throat. I glanced down at my dirty left toe and felt my face flush red. I was sure I still smelled like the Thames.

"Go on, then," he urged. "Is there a problem with the animals, lad?"

"Oh, no, sir. Nothing like that. It's Broad Street."

"Broad Street?" He held a napkin in one hand. I groaned inwardly. I was interrupting his breakfast. Then I thought of Bernie, who was too sick to eat.

I pulled myself together. "Sir, it's the blue death. The cholera has come to Broad Street."

The doctor threw down his napkin and grabbed me by the shoulders. His voice came out huskier than ever. "Are you sure?"

"Y-yes, sir. There can be no doubt of it," I stammered. He shook me a little.

"Your name is Eel, as I recall. So, Eel, how can you be certain?" Dr. Snow queried. "Do you have any idea what the symptoms of cholera look like?"

"Yes, Dr. Snow. I do now," I told him. "I saw one man die of it, and now his wife and little boy are struck. And many more besides."

"You'd better come in," he ordered, letting me loose.

My mouth fell open. But he was already beckoning me inside. "Yes, yes. Come in while I get ready. I have more questions for you."

I stopped to pick up his napkin and trailed behind him,

walking on tiptoe. Where was Mrs. Weatherburn? I could imagine her appearing, taking one sniff of the air, and declaring, "A mudlark is here!"

We passed through a small dining room, and Dr. Snow nodded toward the sideboard. "Have you eaten? Help yourself to toast. If, that is, you can eat while you talk."

I placed the napkin carefully on the sideboard. I didn't want to be accused of stealing it. The sideboard had dishes with enough food for a half-dozen people, not just one man. There were eggs and tomatoes and late-summer strawberries. The toast was warm and buttery. I snatched two pieces, folded them, and stuffed them into my pocket for later.

I looked longingly at the little pot of raspberry jam. No sense in taking the risk of dropping a big blob of jam on Dr. Snow's rich green carpet. Mrs. Weatherburn would want to lock me in the Tower of London for that.

Dr. Snow had gone through to the next room, a small study that faced the street. I stood in the doorway. I could see shelves lined with great, fat books. There was a desk and two large tables piled high with papers. On one sat an instrument I recognized as a microscope.

"So, where did you say it was again?" Dr. Snow was wrapping some cloth around glass vials and packing them into a large black bag.

"In the neighborhood of Broad Street, sir. Not far north of here, across Regent Street, just past the Golden Square."

"Ah yes, I know it," he said. "Go on. When did it begin?"

"Well, I suppose, sir, it was Thursday," I said. "At least that's when Mr. Griggs got very ill."

"And who is Mr. Griggs?" Dr. Snow glanced at me. "Come closer, lad. I can barely hear you if you stay there on the threshold and mumble."

"But, sir, I don't like to. My shoes . . ." I looked down. "Mrs. Weatherburn . . ."

"Ah, quite right. I'm a trial to the good lady myself." He smiled. "Fine. Stay where you are, then, but speak up. You were telling me about Mr. Griggs."

"Mr. Griggs is a tailor at Forty Broad Street, sir. He lives upstairs from his shop with his family," I said. It was hard to talk loudly. These weren't the kind of rooms where a body could feel comfortable shouting.

"That is, I mean to say, he did live there," I went on. "He died on Friday, a bit after noon."

"How do you know this?" Dr. Snow's eyes bored into me.

"I visited him Thursday when he was sick. And also the next day when . . . it happened." I swallowed. "You can ask Reverend Whitehead. He was there too and told us it was the cholera."

I couldn't tell if Dr. Snow believed me, so I plunged on. "That's not all, sir. After that they hung up a yellow flag to warn folks not to come near. They spread out lime too. Nasty-smelling stuff, that is. But they say it keeps the cholera from spreading and helps to clean the air. You know, from the miasma."

"Hmph! Miasma. Cleans the air!" To my surprise, Dr. Snow shook his head in disgust. Then he went on, talking more to himself now. "Cholera. A few blocks away. And I'm just hearing about it now. Well, no wonder. I've had so many cases that I've barely been home these last two days.

"Keep talking, lad," he commanded over his shoulder, still busy with his bag. "Is this Mr. Griggs the only death so far?"

"Oh, no, sir." I thought of all I had seen while helping Charlie the coffin man. "No. It's more like a spark that has caught and now it's a roaring fire."

I hesitated. "I think . . ."

"Go on. You think what?"

"Sir, I believe there must be tens struck down by now, maybe a hundred or more. Folks have gotten sick in the neighborhood all around Broad Street," I said in a rush. "At least, that's what the coffin man and I saw yesterday."

Dr. Snow straightened up to face me, leather bag forgotten. He caught me in a gaze so firm I couldn't get away. But his voice came out soft, as though I were a dog he was afraid to spook. "What made you talk to a coffin man?"

"I did some work for 'im, sir. To earn a few coins."

"What kind of work?"

"Helping load the coffin cart when 'is mate got faint and couldn't stomach it."

"Did you touch the dead yourself?" Dr. Snow rasped, coming closer.

"Not exactly, sir."

"What do you mean, 'not exactly'?" Dr. Snow was close now. He reached out and took me by my shoulders.

"At first we had wooden coffins for the bodies," I explained. "But those ran out. So then the coffin man had to use burlap sacks. But Charlie . . . he didn't make me touch any bodies. He said that wouldn't be fair, me being just thirteen. He did it himself. Usually the family helped."

"Promise me," said Dr. Snow, gripping my shoulders more tightly. "I want you to promise me that you will never do that again. And if you go into the houses where the sick people are, try not to touch anything. Most of all, do not drink the water."

Why was he telling me this? I wondered. Wasn't cholera spread by poisons in the air?

"Sir, about the sick people," I said quickly. I'd have to ask more about the water later. "That's why I'm here. Mr. Griggs had a wife and two children. Mrs. Griggs and little Bernie are both sick. Bernie has lasted more than a day. That's a good sign, isn't it, sir? I mean, does everyone die of it?"

"Many do," said Dr. Snow, who had let me go and was walking back to his desk. "But not all."

At least that meant Bernie might have a chance. "Dr. Snow, please, you have to come."

Dr. Snow no longer seemed to be listening. He finished packing his bag and beckoned me to follow him—this time heading for the front door. "Come along, then."

"That way? Through the front door of your house, sir? I . . . I couldn't. I don't think Mrs.—"

"Now!"

I rushed on tiptoe after him. I glanced behind me. The house was still quiet. It was Sunday. Perhaps Mrs. Weatherburn had gone to church.

I hoped she had, and that she wasn't strolling down Sackville Street on her way home right now—in time to see a mudlark coming out the front door.

CHAPTER THIRTEEN
Dr. Snow's Patient

Dr. Snow walked briskly, snaking through the crowds on Regent Street. I had to hurry to keep up. My mind was working almost as fast as my legs.

I'd done it! The great doctor was on his way to Broad Street. *He'll be able to help Bernie and Mrs. Griggs now,* I thought. *Maybe Dr. Snow can save everyone.*

We veered off Regent Street and passed through the Golden Square. Usually the small park was crowded with courting couples or workers stopping to have a smoke. Now it was empty, except for a pigeon on the statue's head.

The statue depicted a fine-looking fellow, strong and proud. Once, Florrie and I had happened upon Rev. Whitehead sitting in the park. He'd been reading, but when he saw us, he closed his book and greeted us with a friendly smile.

"I like to sit and watch the pigeons enjoying the view from George the Second's head," he remarked, pointing. "Do you know who he was?"

"He was a great king from ages ago, weren't he?" said Florrie.

"Indeed he was, though I am afraid history tells us he had a reputation for being rather mean."

"He seems nice enough," said Florrie. "I think it would be awful to be made into a nasty-looking statue and have to stay like that for hundreds of years." She laughed and reached into her apron pocket for her sketchbook. "Don't move, Mr. Pigeon! I'm going to draw you."

I watched her work. She had a way of frowning when she was concentrating hard, and tossing one braid over her shoulder when it got in her way. "I'd better be careful to smile around you," I said, "or you'll put me into one of your sketches with a big frown on my face."

"You draw well, Florrie," remarked Rev. Whitehead.

"Thank you, sir. I just do it for fun. It would be lovely to make something out of stone or marble, though . . . some-thing that would last," she said thoughtfully, studying the statue. "I'd like to do one thing in my life that would keep on for a long time."

Rev. Whitehead smiled. "Not all of us can make statues.

But I believe the actions we take and the kindnesses we practice endure beyond our own lives."

I hadn't seen Dr. Snow put any medicine in his bag. I did wonder what those glass vials were for. Maybe he would draw blood from Bernie or ask him to spit into one. But as we got closer to Broad Street, Dr. Snow didn't seem interested in Bernie. Instead he wanted to discuss details about the epidemic itself. "Tell me more."

I paused, trying to sort out everything that had happened over the last few days. Dr. Snow seemed to sense I was a bit muddled.

"Just start at the beginning," he suggested. "You mentioned that Mr. Griggs was probably the first to die. Was he also the first to show signs of the disease?"

"I believe so, sir," I answered slowly. "At least, Reverend Whitehead didn't mention anyone else being sick first."

"Go on, Eel," said Dr. Snow. "Can you tell me more about seeing Mr. Griggs after he got sick? What was his condition?"

"His sheets were wet, sir, as though he had . . . well, been sick," I said, panting. Dr. Snow hadn't let up his speed for a second. "There were white particles everywhere, and he was in horrible pain. It was like a wild animal had got hold of his insides and wouldn't let go."

We turned the corner onto Broad Street. "Point out his house, Eel."

"There, sir. It's Number Forty, just across from the Lion Brewery and in front of the pump. Other families share the house too," I told him. "It's not like your street, if you know what I mean."

"Indeed I do," said Dr. Snow.

"Is that what causes the cholera, Dr. Snow? Folks being crowded all together and breathing foul air?" I wanted to know. "Because that's what I heard from . . . well, from everyone."

"It's called the miasma theory—the notion that diseases like cholera are spread by contaminated air," Dr. Snow said. "Miasma is a kind of poisonous vapor, or so people think. This air supposedly contains particles of bad-smelling decaying matter, the kind we find in neighborhoods such as this, where families are crowded together and there is poor sanitation."

I felt hopeful. I'd known Dr. Snow was an expert in chloroform, but it sounded like he might know about cholera too.

"The miasma theory has been around for centuries," Dr. Snow continued. "People, even educated men, have believed it for so long that most are afraid to think in a different way, or consider a new idea."

"But don't you believe in miasma, Dr. Snow?" I asked. "Or do you have a new idea?"

"I do," he said with a sort of laugh. "I've been working on a theory of the spread of cholera for several years now. Although I must admit that no one has paid much attention to it."

"On account of it being new?"

"That's part of it. If people are told something for hundreds of years, it's difficult to change their minds," Dr. Snow explained. "It would help if we could *see* cholera.

"So, although I have gathered a lot of evidence, I need a study that will convince people that my way of thinking is right. In other words, I need more proof," he told me. "Perhaps this trouble here on Broad Street is one way to get it."

What was his theory? I wondered. What sort of proof did he need? And most of all, when would he go up to see Bernie and Mrs. Griggs?

Suddenly Dr. Snow pointed to the Lion Brewery. "Eel, have any of the brewery workers gotten sick?"

"Well, no, I don't think so."

"I imagine they have another source," he muttered to himself.

I had no idea what he was talking about. I rocked back and forth on my heels, looking up at Bernie's window. I'd managed to convince Dr. Snow to come to Broad Street, but so far all he'd done was talk about theories and ask me questions.

"Dr. Snow, please," I said urgently. "Can you—"

Before I could finish, Rev. Whitehead emerged from the door in front of us. His head was bent, and he stopped and drew in a long breath, as if to steady himself.

The reverend's face was so drawn that for an instant I

feared he might be the next victim. But then he wouldn't be upright and walking around, I reminded myself.

"Eel, I'm glad to see you're well," he said, his face lighting up a little.

I glanced at the two men, standing beside one another awkwardly. It was up to me, I realized. I tried to remember the proper manners Mum had taught me long ago.

"Uh . . . uh, Reverend, this is Dr. John Snow," I began.

He nodded his approval at my effort and reached out to shake the doctor's hand. "I'm Henry Whitehead, assistant curate of St. Luke's. I've heard your name, sir, and know of your experiments with chloroform."

Dr. Snow bowed. "My interest is indeed in using gases like chloroform to ease pain. But I've also been a student of cholera for some years, and am just now learning of this epidemic. How many victims have there been so far?"

"By my count, Dr. Snow, more than seventy people have died since Friday afternoon, and there may be more," the reverend replied with a heavy sigh. "I've visited rooms where entire families are suffering together, with no one to help. It is heartbreaking."

"The disease has spread beyond Broad Street, I presume," Dr. Snow said.

"Yes, it has, though it appears to be at its worst right here. I've just come from Peter Street, near Green's Court, not far from where we stand," he told us. "I went into four houses there, and found half the residents of each one struck down by the disease."

He drew a handkerchief from his pocket and wiped his forehead. "I fear there can be no doubt: this stench, this stifling bad air of summer, and the appalling sanitation in some of these houses—all these things are culprits here."

Dr. Snow looked the younger man in the eye. "I know that is what everyone believes. But I must tell you that my studies over the last several years suggest that the miasma theory is wrong. There is another cause of this epidemic."

"Oh?" Rev. Whitehead sounded skeptical.

"I believe cholera results not from breathing bad air, but from ingesting by mouth some morbid material that causes the disease," Dr. Snow replied.

I guessed *ingesting* must mean eating or drinking. But what was "morbid material"?

Rev. Whitehead said nothing. His kind face wore a doubtful expression—about as doubtful as I felt.

"I believe there must be a period of incubation that is quite short, while the poison grows or multiplies in the infected person," Dr. Snow went on, seemingly unaware that at least some of his audience (that is to say, me) was not understanding much of what he said.

"Further, it seems clear to me, though apparently not to others, that since this disease affects the alimentary canal, the poison must enter the person through the mouth."

I frowned, wondering what that was. *Canal* made me think of the river.

"The alimentary canal," Dr. Snow explained. "It's the pathway by which food enters the human body at one end and is expelled at the other."

"Oh," I said. It felt odd to be standing with two gentlemen talking about such things. But if I was embarrassed, the doctor wasn't bothered at all.

"In short, my belief is that cholera is spread by water," the doctor concluded at last. He pointed. "Quite possibly by this very pump."

"Dr. Snow, I doubt it could be from this pump, even if your basic idea could be proved," Rev. Whitehead replied. "The water from the well under the Broad Street pump is known to have a good taste. And it is far less cloudy than that from nearby pumps. Surely it has fewer impurities. How can it be the cause?"

"Sir, I understand why it's easy to think that foul smells mean that miasma is the cause of disease. I also know it is difficult to grasp that water that looks and tastes clean could instead be the culprit," said Dr. Snow. "And it's true that, even if I test the water, I may find nothing."

"What will you do then, Dr. Snow?" Rev. Whitehead wanted to know. "How will you solve what appears to me to be a complete mystery?"

"There are other ways to investigate. My hope is that this epidemic, raging so quickly in such a small neighborhood, will help me build a case that will convince you and others of my theory," said Dr. Snow.

He paused for breath. His next question surprised me.

"Can you tell me, is there a local governance committee for this neighborhood?"

"Why, yes. There is a board of governors for St. James Parish. I understand that the board has formed a special committee to respond to the emergency." Rev. Whitehead added, "In fact, they are meeting on Thursday evening at seven to discuss the outbreak."

"Thursday evening . . . ," Dr. Snow repeated thoughtfully. "And does this committee have any power to take action to help stop this horrible epidemic?"

"Yes indeed," Rev. Whitehead replied. "Already lime has been put in the streets to try to clean the air. Signs have been posted warning the general population of the outbreak. Undertakers have been contacted to bring coffins. What else can be done?"

Dr. Snow stared at the pump before us. "I have an idea that might work, if I can convince the committee to act. And if I can muster enough evidence in time."

"Doctor, your intentions certainly seem honorable," said Rev. Whitehead wearily. "But I fear that epidemics such as this are beyond our poor powers to understand."

"Give me a chance to convince you otherwise," said Dr. Snow. "Like you, I do not want to watch more innocent people die."

"I wish you luck, sir. We all need it. And now good day," said Rev. Whitehead. "I see Dr. Rogers up ahead and must ask him to check on some of my parishioners."

"But what about Bernie?" I put in. "And Mrs. Griggs? How are they?"

"I'm sorry, lad," he said, putting his hand on my shoulder. "I'm afraid Mrs. Griggs is gone. Nor is there much hope for the boy. Florrie Baker and Mrs. Lewis are with him now."

Dr. Snow bent down to open his black bag.

"Can we please go up now, sir?" I asked.

Dr. Snow glanced at me quizzically. "Go up?"

"To see Bernie!" I exclaimed. "Aren't you . . . here to visit patients?"

"Oh, I see. No, I'm sorry. I cannot help your friend or anyone who has already contracted cholera. My patient is a different one," said Dr. Snow. He pointed to the Broad Street pump.

"The pump!" I gasped in disbelief. "This stupid pump isn't going to help Bernie. He's sick now!"

"I can't do anything for your friend," said Dr. Snow softly. "Once someone has cholera, there is little we can do. We don't yet know enough to stop the course of the disease. I can only hope to save those who have not fallen ill."

"But . . . but . . . ," I sputtered, pointing to his bag. "Why did you bring that? I thought you were going to do a test, or that you might have . . . medicine or something."

Dr. Snow unwrapped one of the glass vials. "I am going to

test the water. As I told Reverend Whitehead, I've developed a theory about how cholera spreads, which I feel sure is sound. Now I need clear and definitive proof to convince others.

"The Broad Street epidemic could provide the evidence I must have to make a case that is beyond doubt," the doctor went on. "There is no time to waste. It is Sunday. We have only four days and much to do."

I'd thought Dr. Snow could help Bernie, but he didn't care at all about him—or anyone else. I looked down at his bag and felt like kicking it.

"So you don't have special medicine in there? You're supposed to be one of the best doctors in London, maybe the whole country." I clenched my fists in frustration. "I thought you could make folks better."

"I know how you feel, lad," said Dr. Snow. "I can never forget the first time I watched cholera devastate a community, sweeping through houses like a terrible windstorm.

"The sad truth is that I have no medicine. No one docs—yet. Do I believe that someday we will find a cure and that we can make progress against epidemics like this? Yes, I fervently hope so. But it will take time and work."

I turned away and started to stomp off. Dr. Snow called me back.

"Eel, there is something we can—something we must—do," he said. "This swift, fierce epidemic is a chance to show how the disease spreads."

Dr. Snow's next words startled me. "And I could use your help."

"What can I do? I'm just a mudlark." I was sure he was making fun of me.

"If we can bring evidence to the committee on Thursday night, we might be able to prevent more people from getting sick. We might be able to save lives."

"But . . . but . . . that's not good enough," I cried. "Bernie is dying *now*."

Dr. Snow opened his mouth. I didn't stop to listen.

I scrambled up the stairs and pushed open the door of the room. Florrie had her arm around Betsy, who was sleeping. Bernie lay on a pallet in the corner.

"Oh, Eel," whispered Florrie when she saw me.

Her eyes looked large and frightened, though she wasn't crying. "He's goin', poor little thing. He's calling for his papa. Sometimes he's awake, and then he slips off a bit."

"Have you been all alone?"

"Mrs. Lewis was just here. But she has her own troubles. She lost her baby yesterday," Florrie said. "Fanny weren't even six months old, poor dearie."

She looked behind me at the empty doorway. "You didn't bring 'im, did you?"

I shook my head. "Dr. Snow said there's nothing he can do once someone has it." I felt hot tears sting my eyes. "He's out there, though, down at the pump."

"What's the pump got to do with anything?"

"Dr. Snow thinks the blue death spreads by some kind

of invisible poison in the water, rather than by bad air," I told her.

Florrie stared at me. "Is the water from the Broad Street pump bad somehow?"

"Dr. Snow's not sure yet. He wants to test it," I said. Then I stopped. What if he was right?

"I never drink from there myself," I said slowly, looking at the bucket and ladle in the corner. "But have you drunk from that pump in the last few days?"

"A little." Florrie swallowed hard. "A neighbor came by and brought a jug of milk. Bernie wouldn't touch it, so I gave it to Betsy. But I drank some water."

"Dr. Snow could be wrong," I said, trying to make her feel better. "But it might be best not to drink any more."

Just then Bernie whimpered.

"Go over and talk to him, Eel," Florrie whispered. "He looks up to you something fierce."

Bernie's small hand felt dry as paper. His cracked lips looked sore. His skin had a bluish tint. You could see his ribs heaving up and down from the effort to breathe.

"Don't be scared, Bernie," I said softly. "Your pa's lookin' after you."

Bernie opened his eyes and stared at me. He gave a hoarse gasp. Then his little body gave up fighting.

CHAPTER FOURTEEN
Four Days

I stood in the hot, close room, looking down at Bernie's still form. Anger surged through me. "It ain't fair."

Florrie drew the sheet over Bernie's face. She nodded toward the corner, where Betsy lay curled up with a napping Dilly. "I'm glad I didn't wake 'er. It don't seem right that in three days she's lost her whole family. I hate that I can't do anything. But maybe *you* can, Eel. Maybe you can help your Dr. Snow somehow."

We went into the hall. Florrie said she would fetch Mrs. Lewis and ask her to keep Betsy. "I think she has an aunt somewhere. I 'spect Mrs. Lewis will know how to reach her." Like Rev. Whitehead, she had dark shadows under her eyes from lack of sleep. "I need to get home."

I cleared my throat. "Be careful how you go, Florrie."

"You too, Eel."

Dr. Snow was still standing before the pump, making notes in a small black book. He took one look at my face and said, "I'm sorry, lad."

I stared down at my feet and pushed at a cobblestone with my toe. I wouldn't cry in front of Dr. Snow, not in front of any swell like him.

"Sorry for running off . . . ," I mumbled.

A few families passed by us, but the stream of refugees was a trickle compared to Friday afternoon. I figured most everyone who could leave had already gotten away. I looked into the dark, empty windows around us. Were there still children like Bernie lying inside, suffering, with no one left to help them?

"Eel, I've been studying cholera in other parts of London, but this epidemic is different," Dr. Snow said urgently. "It's come on fast, and is confined to one neighborhood. That makes me suspect a direct link with a single water source.

"I meant what I said. This might be the best chance I'll ever have to prove my theory. And I do need your help."

"But . . . what could I do?"

"I can't stop all my other work. So I need an assistant. You know these streets and the people who live here," Dr.

Snow explained. "More importantly, they know you. You're not a strange fancy doctor they've never seen before."

"True enough. I'll never be a swell like you," I said. Then I shook my head. "But I can't exactly make out what you want me to do."

"Well, for one thing, talk. I will need you to help me visit homes and talk to people."

"You mean, warn them about drinking the water?" I thought of Florrie, and how she had drunk water from the pump.

"Warning will be part of it, yes. We will also need to ask questions to determine if the Broad Street pump really is to blame for the cholera.

"Don't worry. I'll guide you and tell you what to ask," Dr. Snow reassured me.

Then he added, "And naturally, I'll pay you."

Dr. Snow would pay me just to talk to people. I could use the money. But I wouldn't help Dr. Snow for that reason. I would do it for Bernie's sake.

"What do you say, Eel?"

"All right," I agreed. "I'll do it. Though I'm not sure how talking to people can prove anything."

"You'll see," Dr. Snow promised. "But we must start at the beginning. The first thing I want you to do is to close your eyes."

It must be, I thought, a sort of test. Of what, I couldn't say. I didn't know how to pass it either. So I just shut my eyes. What I saw was Bernie's small face, etched with pain, which made me quiver. I had to take a great gulp of air to calm myself.

As I did, Dr. Snow took me by the shoulders and moved me so I was facing a different direction. "All right, now open your eyes and tell me what you see."

What I saw was the Broad Street pump.

"Now, Eel, I want you to pretend you are seeing this neighborhood for the first time," Dr. Snow instructed. "What would you say about this pump? Just tell me everything that pops into your head."

"Well, a pump is one place that people in the neighborhood get their water, though some also get it piped into their houses these days," I said slowly. "It pumps water up from a well, and folks use that water to cook with and, of course, to drink."

He nodded. "Go on."

"Uh . . . this here is the Broad Street pump, but it ain't the only one in the vicinity. Most people use the pump closest to them, though not always. I mean, it's a matter of taste sometimes," I said. "The Broad Street pump is known as a good one; the water isn't too murky. Though I never drank from it when I worked at the Lion."

I stopped and felt my cheeks get hot. "Uh . . . but I don't work there anymore."

"Are you in the habit of drinking from any other pumps around here?" Dr. Snow asked.

I had to think about that for a minute. "Well, I stop at Bridle Street sometimes, or Warwick Street, on account of that pump is near the park in Golden Square. I like to wash off my legs and sit in the sun to dry, especially if I've been mudlarking, which is rather a dirty business."

Dr. Snow smiled. "Can you name some of the other pumps in this area?"

"There's one on Vigo Street. Oh, and there's the Little Marlborough Street pump, but everyone tries to avoid it." I wrinkled my nose. "The water smells awful bad."

"Now, you said you didn't drink from this pump when you worked at the Lion," said Dr. Snow. "Why not?"

"We had our own water, which was delivered from the New River Company to make ale. We had a well too," I said. "I think most of the men—there were about seventy workers—just drank ale. I never got in the habit of stopping at the Broad Street pump because I always had a jug of cold, clear water waitin' for me at the Lion."

"Very good, Eel. Now, what else can you tell me about this neighborhood?"

I frowned up at him. His dark eyes seemed kind enough, but they held a challenge: was I just an ignorant mudlark, or was I worthy of helping in this important work?

"Well, like I said, we have lots of families, squeezed together close, and lots of little shops and businesses too,"

I said. "There's the brewery, of course, and other tailors besides Mr. Griggs. We have a bakery, a furniture maker, a greengrocer, a jeweler, a bonnet maker. I know a shop that sells trimming for ladies' hats, a dressmaker, and an engraver. Oh, and an umbrella maker too.

"Besides the Lion, I guess the Eley Brothers factory is the largest business. They make those percussion caps, the little metal part of a firearm that contains the gunpowder," I said. "Then there's the St. James Workhouse over on Poland Street."

Just thinking about the workhouse made me shudder. Rev. Whitehead and Dr. Snow might be nicer than most swells, but I couldn't trust them with the truth. If they knew it was just Henry and me (and him not even eight years old), they might think the best place for us was that very workhouse. It would feel like being in prison, stuck in with hundreds of men, women, and children, all put in separate dormitories and made to do what everyone else did, day after day.

All at once I thought of something. "Dr. Snow, there must be more than five hundred folks in that workhouse, but Reverend Whitehead hasn't mentioned anything about the cholera there, and Charlie the coffin man didn't need to go near it."

"Hmmm, interesting," mused Dr. Snow. "You're doing well, Eel. Anything else?"

In front of us, a hearse stopped, pulled by a horse so skinny its ribs showed through. Two men, with handkerchiefs tied over their mouths, brought a wooden box into a house across the way.

I took a breath and kept talking, almost as if my life depended on it. And perhaps it did.

"Excellent observations," said Dr. Snow when I'd finally run out of words. "Now, while you were with your friend, I drew some samples from the pump. I'll take them home to look at under the microscope. Though I'm afraid that up to now, I haven't been able to see cholera material in water. No one has."

"So what will you do to prove the cholera comes from water?"

"We will have to use other means to prove my theory. We'll have to rely on the Four *W*'s."

I frowned. "Never heard of them."

"These are four questions that must occupy us in trying to understand—and stop—this outbreak. If we ask the right questions, we may just find the answers. Can you guess what they are?"

I must have looked bewildered because the doctor smiled and said, "Just use your common sense. That's always the best place to start."

"Uh . . ." I hated to look stupid in front of Dr. Snow. I had to come up with something. "Well, could one of those *W*'s be *What*? Because we want to know: *What* is going on?"

Dr. Snow beamed, just as he had when I'd captured his

guinea pig the first time we met. It made him look younger somehow. "Yes indeed. We must start by asking, What is going on? What is the disease?"

"Well, that's easy. It's cholera: the blue death."

Dr. Snow nodded. "We are sure it is cholera in this epidemic. But doctors may not always know. Many times in history, people were confronted with a disease and did not understand what it was. Now, can you guess what the next question is?"

I stared blankly. Then I noticed that Dr. Snow had begun looking curiously at the houses, craning his neck as if to peer inside. This must be some kind of hint.

"*Who?*" I exclaimed. "The second question we should ask is, *Who* is getting sick?"

Dr. Snow nodded. "Very good. Go on."

I kept thinking. What else would I want to know if I were Dr. Snow?

"Well, seems like you might want to ask *where* folks are," I began slowly. "*Where* do the people who are getting sick live?"

"And not just where they live, but where they work or go to school," Dr. Snow agreed. "Even where people go to eat or drink can be important."

I counted them on my fingers: *What? Who? Where?* . . . I tried to think of another *W.* I shook my head. "I give up."

"*When* did they fall ill?" Dr. Snow said, beginning to walk off.

I turned over the Four *W*'s in my mind. *What? Who? Where? When?*

"Dr. Snow, I think you're missing one," I said, hurrying to catch up. "Maybe it should be the Five *W*'s. Maybe we should also ask *Why?*

"Because that's really what we want to know in the end, ain't it? *Why* are ordinary folks getting sick with this awful disease that can kill a body in a single day?"

Dr. Snow turned to me. "Eel, you've hit the nail on the head. Until we understand *why,* we cannot stop cholera from spreading through this or any other neighborhood like a fire out of control.

"I'm rather impressed, lad. You have the makings of a good investigator. Let's go home. We have a lot of work to do in four days."

Home. The word gave me a start. I'd almost forgotten about my own problems, what with thinking about Bernie and the Five *W*'s and all this talk of theories.

I would have to tell Dr. Snow more about the Lion, I decided.

"There's just one thing, sir," I began. "Like I mentioned, I used to work at the Lion Brewery. I lost my situation there last week. It wasn't my fault, I swear. I'm honest. I was falsely accused of stealing."

"Go on."

"But that means I don't have anywhere to live right now." I paused. "So I was wondering . . . do you think I might sleep in your shed, at least for a few days?"

I held my breath.

"Well, that seems reasonable," he said. "Mind you, I'll

have to speak with Mrs. Weatherburn. She runs a tight ship, as you may have noticed. You'll have meals too. And I suppose we should come to an understanding about your wages."

I waited, hoping it would be enough to pay Mrs. Miggle.

"This will be different work from what you've done before, Eel," he went on. "Oh, there's physical work: long hours of walking up and down the neighborhood and knocking on doors."

"I'm strong and I don't get tired," I put in eagerly.

Dr. Snow waved a hand. "But more than that, this work will require all your faculties: your eyes, your hearing, your brain—and a pen. But wait, you probably don't read or write."

"Actually, I do," I told him. "I went to a day school till I was ten, and then a ragged school—when I could—up until . . . up until last year. I know my numbers too."

"Excellent. We must present to the committee in four days' time. But the work won't end there. It will take me weeks after that, if not months, to finish a thorough study," Dr. Snow explained.

"You already pay me two shillings a week now, sir," I reminded him, "to clean the cages and feed your animals."

"Do I? All right, then. I'll add four more. What do you say to six shillings a week, plus breakfast and dinner?"

Six shillings. Breakfast and dinner. It would be more than enough.

"Thank you, sir. I'm . . . I'm very grateful." Then I thought of Mrs. Miggle. "Do you think, Dr. Snow, that I might be paid a part of my wages by Friday morning? It's on account of a previous commitment."

Dr. Snow's eyes twinkled. "Do you mean to tell me you're in debt, Eel?"

"Nothing like that, sir."

To my surprise, Dr. Snow pulled three shillings out of his pocket and dropped them into my hand. "Here's an advance. You'll have three more on Friday morning. Believe me, young man, you will work for it."

PART THREE

The Investigation

In most of the Broad Street houses, every floor, and in some every room, contained a separate family. It was, therefore, in many cases not enough to take the word of the ground-floor people with regard to the habits of the house. Each family had to be visited, and, as far as possible, each member of the family conversed with.

—Rev. Henry Whitehead,
"The Broad Street Pump: An Episode in the Cholera Epidemic of 1854,"
Macmillan's Magazine (December 1865)

CHAPTER FIFTEEN
In Which I Am Given
a Daunting and Important Task

Monday, September 4

The next morning, I woke long before dawn. First off, I reached into my pocket. The three shillings Dr. Snow had given me were still there, plus the two I'd earned working with Charlie the coffin man.

As it got light, Dr. Snow's animals began to stir. I was wide awake too. I decided to bring Mrs. Miggle the two shillings I owed from last week. She'd be glad to have the money. I had another reason too: losing Bernie had made me anxious about Henry. I knew my little brother wasn't anywhere near the cholera outbreak. Still, I'd feel better if I checked on him.

Slipping out of the shed, I soon left Dr. Snow's quiet neighborhood behind. I made my way along winding streets and alleys, darting around horses and carts on the way to market (and being careful to avoid fresh piles of dung).

Mrs. Miggle was so surprised to see me (and especially my shillings) that she gave Henry and me two hot cross buns each to stuff in our pockets.

"Come on, then. I'll walk you to school today," I told Henry.

"Ain't it too dangerous, Eel? Because of *him*?"

I poked Henry in the ribs, which made him giggle. "Just this once. We'll be careful."

"Do you miss her, Eel?" Henry wanted to know as we walked along.

I nodded. "Of course. Don't you?"

Henry bit his lip and nodded. "I do. But . . . I can't see her clear in my mind anymore."

"That's not your fault. You were still six when she died," I told him gently. I thought of the sketches Florrie had made for Betsy. At least Betsy would have something to help her remember *her* mother's face.

"Did . . . did 'e love her, Eel?"

"Of course Pa loved her!"

"Not Pa. I hardly remember him," Henry said. "You know who I mean. *Him*."

"No," I told Henry firmly. "He didn't. Bill Tyler is a villain, and don't you forget it. He married our mum because she was beautiful and sweet. And she agreed because she hoped that he would take care of us. But that ain't what happened. He never loved her. And you can be sure our stepfather never loved us."

I grabbed Henry's arm. "And that's why, if you ever see him coming, you got to run. You understand me? You run as fast and hard as you can and you get away from him. You can't trust him."

"He weren't so mean to me . . . ," Henry protested, trying to pull out of my grasp.

I pinched his thin arm so hard he began to whimper. "Listen to me, Henry. Promise me you'll run if you ever see him. Will you do that?"

Henry was nearly trembling with fear now, and I was sorry for that. But he was too trusting.

"I promise." He sniffled. "But how long do I have to stay at Mrs. Miggle's? Why can't I come live with you?"

"Because you can't," I said shortly.

"Maybe I'll run away and find you," he said, his lower lip trembling.

"Henry, don't say that!" I hissed. "You gotta stay with Mrs. Miggle, you hear me?"

Henry threw his arms around me and buried his face in my shirt. "Sorry, Eel," he mumbled. "I'll be good. I just . . . I miss you."

"I know," I whispered. "Everything will turn out fine, I promise. Go on now."

And he scurried away into school.

I was still worried about Henry all the way back to Sackville Street. How was I going to make things better? Why couldn't Mrs. Miggle be nicer?

I was so caught up in my own thoughts I didn't even hear Mrs. Weatherburn come up behind me as I worked in the shed. She cleared her throat. I mumbled, "Mornin'."

"Young man, is that how you say good morning to your betters?"

"No, ma'am." I gave a little bow. "Good morning, Mrs. Weatherburn."

"Hmph." Clearly, my performance was not entirely satisfactory.

"The doctor says you are to come into the kitchen for your breakfast and then to his study when you're done," she ordered.

Mrs. Weatherburn put her hands on her hips, looking me up and down. Her white apron was as bright as a cloud. "And brush the straw and dirt from your sleeves before you step into the house."

"Yes, ma'am."

Inside, she'd set a place for me at the small table in the kitchen. There was tea, toast, and an egg sticking straight up in a cup. I stared at it.

"Take its head off," she instructed.

"Beg your pardon, ma'am?"

"With your spoon. Take the top of the egg off with your spoon," she told me shortly.

We'd never had eggs in cups like this at home. Mrs. Weatherburn watched my struggles for a minute, then simply strode across the kitchen to do it for me. She made me so nervous I felt sure the egg I did manage to swallow would curdle in my stomach.

"More tea?" she asked.

"Please, ma'am. Thank you," I said, my mouth full of toast. Not only toast but jam. Real raspberry jam. This time I hadn't been able to resist.

"I've been Dr. Snow's housekeeper for a good while now," she remarked as I chewed. "A kinder gentleman you'll never meet."

"Yes, ma'am," I managed. That was clearly the safest answer.

"He's very dedicated to *science*," she said, emphasizing the word with reverence.

"Yes, ma'am. I'm sure he is." Was she going to give me yet another long lecture about Dr. Snow being a genius?

"And as I've told you before, I'll not have him taken advantage of in any way. Especially not by a greedy street urchin."

"But, Mrs. Weatherburn," I protested, putting down my mug of tea. I hoped she wouldn't see that my hand was shaking a little. "I'm not . . . I wouldn't . . ."

For answer, she just eyed me coolly and picked up my

plate. There was one crust left, and I would've eaten it if I could have.

Dr. Snow appeared in the doorway. "Ah, there you are, loitering over your tea. Tomorrow, Eel, present yourself at six-thirty. We don't have a moment to lose. For now, follow me."

I felt even more nervous as I trailed the doctor to his study. What if I bumped into something? I felt Mrs. Weatherburn's eyes boring into my back. I stopped in the doorway. "Sir, are you sure it's all right for me to come in? It seems like a great library—or a grand museum."

Dr. Snow chuckled and waved me closer. "Come in, come in. I want to show you something. Put your eye here."

He gestured toward the microscope on the table.

"It's a beautiful microscope," I said, venturing closer. "It's a bit like a church organ, ain't it, sir?"

Dr. Snow seemed surprised. "What makes you say that?"

"Well, it's mysterious-like," I said. "Just looking at it makes you scratch your head, trying to figure out exactly what it might do. But I expect if you know how to use it, then it ain't a mystery at all."

And then, without thinking, I said, "Mum had a pianoforte once."

Dr. Snow stared at me for a long minute, as if he thought I might say more, but I clammed up.

He was still expecting me to look through the microscope. Bending to the instrument, I put one eye to the glass piece and squinted the other one shut.

"Can you tell what you are seeing?"

"Not really. Though I can guess it's water that you got from the Broad Street pump." I glanced up at him. "Have you found it, sir? Can you see the cholera poison in this water?"

"No, I can find nothing unusual," Dr. Snow said. "Later I'll bring a sample to my colleague Dr. Arthur Hassall, who has a more powerful microscope."

He began to pace back and forth behind his desk. "But even then, we may learn nothing. For while I believe there must be some substance in the water—some kind of poisonous material—that causes the cholera, it may be too small for us to see."

"Could it be floating in the air too, Dr. Snow?" I asked. "The cholera poison, I mean."

"As I mentioned yesterday, my work in this area leads me to believe that whatever causes the disease is ingested."

"On account of the . . . uh, the canal." For the life of me, I couldn't remember its name.

"Alimentary canal, yes. The symptoms of the blue death are vomiting and diarrhea, which are usually caused by eating or drinking something bad," Dr. Snow said. "Now we just have to prove it to the committee."

"Sir, about that," I said hesitantly. "I was just wondering: what do we want the committee to *do*?"

"Ah, I haven't explained that, have I?" Dr. Snow exclaimed. "It's quite simple, lad. We want them to take the handle off the Broad Street pump."

As it turned out, Dr. Snow wouldn't be able to start gathering evidence right away. "I have a tooth extraction to attend this morning," he explained. "After that I will take the samples to Dr. Hassall for him to look at."

"What about me? Am I supposed to start talking to people all on my own?"

"Not yet. First you are going to make a map," Dr. Snow instructed.

"That sounds . . . important."

He laughed. "Don't worry. It will only be in pencil. I will undoubtedly do one in pen later, when I write up my final paper on our investigation.

"But we must start somewhere, Eel," he concluded. "And I believe I can trust you to begin."

Trust. The word stuck with me like a good, hearty breakfast. Not that I'd had many breakfasts as fine as the one Mrs. Weatherburn had given me that morning.

There was hardly anyone left who trusted me, except for Henry and Florrie. And after this morning, even Henry seemed to doubt me. As for grown-ups, well, Mr. Griggs was gone now. And the kindest men at the Lion Brewery, Abel Cooper and Mr. Edward Huggins, most likely had come to believe I was a thief. Maybe when the epidemic was over, I could try to explain what had happened.

For now, I felt the weight of the task the doctor had given

me. Dr. Snow was depending on me. And that counted for something.

He handed me a notebook and pencil.

"Include all the streets around Broad Street," he instructed. "And be sure to mark the location of the public water pumps."

"My friend Florrie Baker is a lot better artist than I am," I said, looking at the blank white pages dubiously.

"Ask her to help if you like," he said. "We're not creating art, though. The key is to make the map clear and readable. And most of all, accurate."

Now, it's one thing to be able to find your way around London, and quite another to make a map on paper. I'd already crumpled up two pages of scribbled lines when I presented myself at Florrie's door on Berwick Street.

She opened it herself, looking a little less tired than she had the day before. I explained about the map and showed her my third attempt. "I think I need help."

She took one look and burst out laughing. "I'd say so, Eel. You're supposed to be drawin' streets, not wanderin' streams. And Broad Street may be called that, but it's not that wide. On your map, Broad Street looks like the Thames!"

"So . . . can you help me?"

But if I thought Florrie would do it all herself while I

stood by and watched, I was wrong. "I'll draw the lines," she told me, "but you'll need to help with the street names."

We decided to begin in Golden Square, which most folks thought of as the heart of the neighborhood. "If Dr. Snow is a scientist, he's going to want his map to be precise," Florrie said, opening the notebook to a clean sheet. "How large an area does it need to cover?"

"Pretty big, I think. Let's go as far as Hanover Square, which is past Regent Street to the west. We can go south to Piccadilly Circus, east to Soho Square, and just past Oxford Street to the north," I suggested.

"All right. Let's put Broad Street just about in the center of our map. Now, to be precise, we should make Regent Street wide and other streets, like Golden Place and Angel Court, small and narrow. You can help with that part too, Eel."

"How so?"

Florrie grinned. "You can count, can't you?"

So that's what I did. For hours Florrie had me count my steps going across roads, and up and down them too, while she carefully sketched a map across two large sheets of paper. It was hot, and my feet got tired. But Florrie insisted that we include every lane and court: Hopkins Street, Duck Lane, Portland Mews, Dufours Place, and many more besides.

Everywhere we went, especially close to Broad Street, we noticed the same thing: the streets were eerily quiet.

Most families had left; the shops were closed. All because of the blue death.

"Put a mark right there for the pump," I said, looking over Florrie's shoulder as we stood on Bridle Street. "We don't want to forget that. Dr. Snow said it will be important to the investigation."

She stopped to shake out her hand, which was cramped from holding the pencil for so long. She wiped sweat from her forehead with a corner of her apron.

"You haven't been drinking the water anymore, have you?" I asked, noticing how pale her face was. "I mean, Dr. Snow's not sure the Broad Street pump is bad, but just in case . . ."

"I haven't. And I told my parents and Nancy and Danny to stop," she said. "But they didn't believe me. Nancy said the water from Broad Street has always tasted better than water from any other pump. She didn't understand how it could be bad. Still, I dumped out her bucket and walked all the way across Oxford Street to the pump on Berners Street. Nancy said I was daft."

"It's good that you did that. Dr. Snow could be right." We were walking along Berwick Street now. In the distance I saw a horse and cart with coffins loaded in the back. Charlie must still be at work. The streets were almost deserted, but that didn't mean the outbreak was over. How many more people had died these last few days? I wondered.

"Listen, you've done most of the work here, Florrie.

When I get paid, I'll give you one of my shillings for this," I offered. "You've earned it."

"That's all right, I'm glad to help." Seeing the empty streets of our neighborhood had made her angry and sad. "I hate this Great Trouble. We have to make it stop.

"But you can buy me an Italian ice anytime," she added with a grin.

At her doorstep, Florrie handed me the map. It really was beautiful.

"Florrie, remember how you said you wanted to make something that would last a long time?" I asked. "Well, I think you might just have done it."

CHAPTER SIXTEEN
Dilly

Tuesday, September 5

Tuesday morning I did a thorough job with the cages and washed all the water dishes. When everything was clean, top to bottom, I stepped back to look. I was proud of my work.

I wasn't just a mudlark anymore, or even a messenger boy in a brewery. I was a real assistant to a famous scientist and investigator (even if I'd needed help from Florrie with my first assignment).

I imagined myself showing Florrie around the menagerie again. "These creatures help advance scientific progress, Miss Baker," I'd say, trying not to sound too puffed up. "Our experiments help us discover the Five *W*'s, which will make it possible to prevent disease."

Suddenly I felt a tap on my shoulder. I wheeled around to find Dr. Snow looking at me with an amused expression. My face flushed. Had I spoken out loud?

"Good morning, Eel," he said, handing me a meat pie wrapped in brown paper. "Mrs. Weatherburn has packed this for you. Let's start walking."

"Where are we . . . ," I began. Then I answered my own question. "Wait, I know. We're going back to the Broad Street pump."

It was, I guessed, only a half mile to Broad Street from Dr. Snow's house. With the doctor walking briskly, as usual, we were there in minutes. Dr. Snow had brought his black bag. When he opened it, I saw that he'd packed Florrie's map, which I'd dropped off with Mrs. Weatherburn the night before.

I held my breath as he turned the map this way and that, checking the names of the streets. I'd tried to spell them right and hoped I hadn't made too many mistakes.

"Excellent work, Eel," he said finally. "You've got a good eye for detail. It appears all the side streets are drawn accurately."

"Florrie Baker did that, sir," I told him. "I just did the lettering."

Then I asked a question that had been on my mind all the time we'd been working on the map. "What's next, Dr.

Snow? How will this map help us solve the mystery of the blue death?"

Before Dr. Snow could answer, a stout woman in a black dress bustled out from Mr. Griggs's shop, pulling Betsy by the hand.

Betsy was crying, her cheeks splotched with tears. She was trying to hold on to Dilly. But Dilly broke away, barking feverishly and running in frantic circles.

"Off with you," cried the woman. "I wouldn't be surprised if dirty creatures like you were the cause of this horror."

"I want Dilly." Betsy sobbed harder. She ran to me then, throwing her arms around my legs. Her whole body trembled.

"Hullo, Betsy. What's happened?" I looked at the woman. "Who are you?"

"I'm 'er aunt from Lant Street, though why it's any of your business, I can't say," she grumbled, shifting a pillowcase stuffed with clothes from one shoulder to the other.

"That's over in the Borough, south of the river, ain't it?"

"That's right. She'll be living with us now," the woman said. "I hope she's a strong 'un and not afraid of hard work. My husband's a cabbie and needs help with the 'orse and muckin' out the stall we rent for it."

Betsy's aunt pulled her niece away from me. Dilly kept barking wildly.

"It's all right, Dilly." I managed to grab the leather collar

Mr. Griggs had gotten for her. I remember how he'd given the shoemaker a nice wool vest for it. Dilly stopped and panted, her pink tongue hanging out one side of her mouth.

Dr. Snow stepped forward, his voice husky and low. He made a little bow in front of Betsy's aunt and extended his hand. "Dear lady, it's so good of you to open your home and heart to your poor niece. I hope this small gift may help ease your sorrow."

I realized he was holding out a pound note. Betsy's aunt made a curtsy and took a deep breath. "That's very kind of you, sir. My brother was good to me, and I can't rightly desert his little orphan now," she said in a softer tone.

All at once, she let out a loud hooting sound and began to sob, fat tears running down her chapped red cheeks.

Betsy spoke up, trying to be heard over her aunt's wails. "Eel, I'm happy to go with my aunt. I promise to be a good girl for her. But . . . can you take Dilly? Please?"

I glanced at Dr. Snow. Keeping Dilly might mean he'd fire me. Feeding a dog wasn't part of our bargain. He watched me silently. I couldn't read his expression. But I couldn't let Betsy down.

"Betsy's father, Mr. Griggs, was kind to me," I told him. "He gave me extra work when I needed it. He found Dilly as a pup. I'll feed her out of my pay, I promise. And she won't bother your menagerie."

Betsy's aunt was still puffing and hooting. I waited. Betsy waited. I think even Dilly waited, sitting on her haunches very prettily now and looking up at Dr. Snow expectantly.

"She had better not go after my rabbits," he said at last. Then he grinned.

I knelt and cupped my hands around Betsy's face. "I'll take good care of Dilly," I promised. "We'll come visit you on Lant Street sometime soon. It's just across the river, after all. You know how Dilly likes a good walk."

Betsy hiccuped loudly. "Don't lose her, Eel. And be sure to scratch her ears the way she likes."

Then she bent down and buried her face in the dog's fur, whispering some secret message. Betsy squared her shoulders and put her hand into her aunt's large one. "I'm ready now, Aunt."

Dr. Snow watched them head down Broad Street.

"Her mum and dad would be proud o' her," I said. "Real proud."

I felt Dr. Snow's hand on my shoulder. "And wherever your parents are, lad, I expect they would be proud of you too."

Dilly whined and walked in a circle for a while. Finally she rested her body against my leg and leaned into me with a great sigh. *You'll have to do,* she seemed to be saying.

First a cat, now a dog. I was beginning to wonder if I had an invisible sign around my neck that only four-legged creatures could see: Takes Unwanted Animals.

Dr. Snow leaned down to scratch behind Dilly's ears. She rolled over to have her belly rubbed. "You call her Dilly, eh? She looks like a border collie crossed with a spaniel of some kind. Reminds me of a dog we had when I was a boy."

I looked at him in surprise. Dr. Snow was a dog lover, after all!

"Well, we've dallied enough here, lad," he went on, straightening up. "We have an errand in Somerset House. It'll be a good walk. How would you like that, Miss Dilly?"

Dilly looked up at him and gave two sharp barks. Now, if only she could charm Mrs. Weatherburn. Somehow I didn't think that would be quite so easy.

When we got to Somerset House, I stopped in my tracks and whistled. "It's so grand. Like a palace."

Dr. Snow grinned. "It was once. In fact, the history of Somerset House goes back to the mid-1500s, though the building and its uses have changed many times since then."

Dr. Snow paused before some stone steps.

"In here," he instructed. "Dilly will have to wait outside."

"You want me to come too?"

"Royalty doesn't live here now," he explained with a laugh. "This is the General Register Office, where the City of London keeps its records of births and deaths."

I told Dilly to wait and followed Dr. Snow.

"My colleague William Farr can help us get a list of all those from St. James and St. Anne's Parishes who have died since Friday," he explained as we entered the building.

He stopped in front of a door. "Here we are. Mind you look sharp and pay attention."

"John, I was just saying that we would see you before the week was out." A portly gentleman with a graying beard came forward to greet Dr. Snow with a smile. Behind him several clerks were bent over desks. "No doubt you're here because of the outbreak in Soho."

Dr. Snow shook his hand and told him, "It's practically on my doorstep, William. I'm putting my other work aside as much as I can to look into this terrible business."

Dr. Farr drew out a ledger from under a counter and began to page through it. "Ah, here we are. For that part of Soho, there were eighty-three deaths from Thursday through Saturday, with all but four of those on Friday and Saturday.

"Now, this is interesting," Dr. Farr said, frowning. "It's certainly a substantial increase above normal."

"Seventy-nine in just *two* days," I cried, unable to stop myself.

"The total is probably twice that by now, young man. Nor do we have reports from the nearby hospitals yet. I wouldn't be surprised to see the death toll reach five hundred by the end of this week," said Dr. Farr. Then he turned to Dr. Snow. "Is this young urchin with you, John?"

"As a matter of fact, he is," Dr. Snow answered cheerfully. "Meet my new assistant. He goes by the name of Eel."

I blushed. Assistant! If only Mum were here so I could tell her.

"Another of your experiments, I presume," Dr. Farr teased.

"In fact, Eel has a well-developed sense of curiosity and is quite tenacious." Dr. Snow smiled at me.

"Curiosity is an admirable trait for an investigator," Dr. Farr said. Then he did something rather surprising. He leaned over the counter and peered at me closely. "Odd. I could swear there is something familiar about the boy. Such extraordinary eyes, almost black."

My stomach lurched. Could Dr. Farr have heard about me from Fisheye Bill? But no. That couldn't be. Dr. Farr held one of the most important positions in London. He wouldn't know someone like Fisheye Bill Tyler.

"Well, perhaps it will come to me later," he said, giving himself a little shake. "At any rate, young man, as a friend of Dr. Snow, you are always welcome here. I hope you will endeavor to deserve his confidence. And I imagine he has told you all about his theory on the spread of cholera."

"You mean about the water, sir?"

Dr. Snow opened his mouth, ready to launch into an explanation. Then we both saw Dr. Farr's wink. He put up his hands.

"No need to lecture, my friend. I'm not convinced that you are right, John. Not yet," Dr. Farr said. "But my office will help any way we can. This is certainly a most alarming death toll in such a short time. Far worse than we normally see when cholera raises its nasty head."

Dr. Snow nodded. "Just so. And I do need your assistance. I'd like a list of the names of these eighty-three dead, along with their addresses."

"We have the records, of course. Unfortunately, though, I'm rather short of staff today," said Dr. Farr. "Can your lad write a clear hand? I'd be happy to have him stay and undertake the task."

"What do you say, Eel? You did all right with lettering yesterday. Can you handle a pen?"

"I'm a bit out of practice, sir. But . . . I can do it," I replied. If I failed, Dilly and I might be looking for another place to stay a lot sooner than expected.

I can't get used to a soft life, I reminded myself. *There won't always be tea and toast with jam for a mudlark.*

Dr. Snow tore out several pages from his notebook and handed them to me. "Eel, I want a list, clean and precise. Include the victim's name, date of death, age, and address. Is that clear?"

I nodded. "Yes, sir, but . . ."

"But what?"

"You didn't quite finish with the explanation, sir," I said hesitantly. "And it would help for me to understand. Are we . . . going to write all their names on our map?"

"Ah, good question." Dr. Snow moved toward the door. "I'll meet you at the Broad Street pump at noon. I expect your list to be complete. Then you shall have your answer."

"Dr. Snow," I said as he put his hand on the wooden doorknob. "If you could . . . just remind Dilly to wait."

"I'll do better than that," Dr. Snow said with a smile. "I'll take her with me on my errand. Will she come, do you think?"

"Yes, sir." I grinned. "I'm sure she will."

After he had closed the door, I wiped my sweaty palms on my pants. I felt nervous being left with Dr. Farr and his stern-looking clerks.

Luckily, Mrs. Weatherburn had washed my shirt and pants. I might still feel like a mudlark on the inside, but at least I didn't smell like one. I sat down at the table that Dr. Farr had asked someone to clear for me and thought suddenly of my father.

Pa had been a respectable man, a clerk in an office, though I wasn't sure where it had been or exactly what he did. I'd only been nine when he died, and now Mum wasn't here to ask.

Still, it felt good to remember that I *was* the son of a clerk.

I can do this, I thought as I found the first name on the ledger and took up my pen. And so I began.

CHAPTER SEVENTEEN
Following the Trail

I t took more than two hours to make the list of dead people. My hand was cramped by the time I made my way back to Soho. The muscles in my back ached. I had a headache and my stomach was growling. Writing was hard work.

I found Dr. Snow standing in front of the Broad Street pump with his arms folded, Dilly napping at his feet. "Ah, here's my assistant!" he greeted me cheerily. "Do you have the list?"

I handed it to him, my heart beating hard. I'd tried my best, thinking of my father and glad that Mum had taught me well.

Someone else had come to mind as I'd worked on the

list: Mr. Edward Huggins from the Lion Brewery. He'd had faith in me too. Now he probably believed I'd stolen from the business. I hadn't seen him since that horrible day. If I ever did again, maybe I could get up enough courage to tell him the truth.

Dr. Snow scanned the list. "Excellent. Looks complete. Let's get to it."

"What are we going to do?"

"Knock on doors."

We stopped before a house at the corner of Broad and Berwick. Dr. Snow pulled a small notebook and pen out of his pocket and handed them to me.

"We'll start here. You write down the particulars while I conduct the interviews," he instructed. "Once you see what to do, we can separate and get more done. Now, what information do you think we shall want to record about those who died?"

"Well, I guess we should start by making sure the list is right and the name of the victim and the age are correct," I ventured.

"Yes, very good," approved Dr. Snow. "Age is a clue to help us learn who is dying from the cholera. Are children and young people affected more than older ones? Asking these questions can help us find a pattern."

I wiped my sweaty palms on my pants. I was starting to feel jittery. I remembered how hard it had been to carry the victims away in coffins. Now I would be going back into the same houses, talking to people who'd lost sons and daughters, husbands and wives.

"What are some of the other questions we need to ask?" Dr. Snow was saying.

"Well, we have a list of the days the people died," I began slowly, trying to remember the Five *W*'s. "But it doesn't tell us *when* they got sick."

Another thought occurred to me. "We should ask about symptoms, and *what* caused each person's death. We want to be sure it was the blue death."

Dr. Snow nodded his encouragement. "Very good, Eel."

I wasn't sure if the Five *W*'s had to be in a certain order, but Dr. Snow didn't seem to mind my rambling. "And we should ask *where* they worked or went to school."

"And what else?" Dr. Snow prompted.

What else? I didn't know. All that writing had worn me out. Maybe because I'd recognized so many of the victims' names. They were my neighbors, and kids like me that I'd seen on the street every day. Dr. Snow should just tell me the answers to all his questions.

"Take your time, Eel," he said. "It will come to you. We want to know where people . . ."

". . . get their water!" I finished. This, I realized, was the most important thing.

"But I *can* warn them not to drink the water from the Broad Street pump?"

"Yes, we should warn them. But be prepared: most

people won't listen," Dr. Snow cautioned. "They believe what they can smell and taste. The air is foul; the water from Broad Street tastes good. It looks clear, and it's certainly less murky than the water from some of the other wells nearby."

"Even Dr. Farr doesn't believe your theory," I said.

"Someday he will," said Dr. Snow with fierce determination.

"How will we show all this on the map?" I wondered.

Dr. Snow spread out the map Florrie and I had made. "As we visit each family, we need to ask not just about the person you have on the list, but about every person who has died in that household."

"You mean, in case other people have died since Saturday?"

"Yes. Then, on the spot on the map where the house is, we will make a little black mark, a rectangle, for each victim."

"A mark in the shape of a coffin," I said softly.

"Exactly." Dr. Snow nodded.

"I'm not sure I understand."

"Take this house in front of us," Dr. Snow said. "For each death at this address, we make a mark on the map. Some addresses will end up with three or four marks beside them; others, one or two. Or none."

I nodded. "But . . . how will this help us convince the committee and prove your theory?"

"Ah, well, if my hypothesis is correct and there is one source of contamination causing the disease, I believe that when we are done, our map will show that most of the deaths are clustered around a single point. I think you can guess what that is."

I could. "The Broad Street pump."

By late afternoon, I'd been doing interviews on my own for several hours. Every time I knocked on a door, my heart pounded. I never knew what I might find behind those shuttered windows and closed doors. The neighborhood might be almost deserted now, but there were still folks fighting for their lives.

Maybe it was easier for Dr. Snow, who had done this work before in different parts of London, in other epidemics. He was also a grown-up and a physician. He didn't know the families the way I did either. I might not remember everyone's name, but I recognized faces. And those faces were full of sorrow and fear.

My first interview without Dr. Snow was one of the hardest. I knocked nervously, half hoping no one would answer. The door swung open and a boy of about four stood there. He reminded me of Henry, with large, dark eyes and pale skin.

"Hullo there," I said. "Is your mum in?"

From behind him, a woman called out in an angry voice, "What do you want? We've trouble enough, if you've come begging."

"No, ma'am. I'm helping Dr. John Snow," I explained.

"He's got some questions he'd like me to ask you about the cholera outbreak."

I took a breath. This next part was harder. "I'm . . . sorry to hear your family has been struck with it."

She sighed heavily and glanced behind her, where a young girl lay on a pallet on the floor.

"Milly's resting now, so you better be quick," she said in a low voice. "I lost my husband, Jack, on Saturday. Milly . . . she's been holding on since Sunday night."

"It won't take long, ma'am," I said, making notes in my book. "Could you tell me where your family gets water?"

"Why, from the Broad Street pump, of course," she said at once. "It's just round the corner. Milly usually fetches it."

"Did your husband . . . that is to say, has anyone in your family been drinking water from the pump lately?"

"Yes . . . ," she began, and then she stopped. A frown creased her brow. "Now, why are you asking about water? I thought the cholera was caused by bad air."

"Most people do think that. But Dr. Snow believes it might be from the water. That's why what you're telling me will help," I said. I repeated my question. "Do you recall whether you all drank from the pump last week?"

She glanced back at the still form behind her. "I expect Milly did, and Jack, my husband. But I was gone a good part of the week. My sister lives in Southwark, and she's been feelin' poorly since her youngest was born."

"And you went to see her?" I prompted. The woman

nodded and pulled the little boy toward her. He hid his head in her skirts.

She continued, "I took my boy with me and left Milly to keep house for her pa. She's a responsible girl for twelve. We come back Friday night to find Jack struck. He was gone the next day. And then Milly got it.

"The little one and I, we're not sick. And here you are, asking about the water," she said thoughtfully. "Was the pump water poisoned, then? It looks so clear, compared to what we get in the pipes."

"Dr. Snow believes the water from the Broad Street pump may be the cause," I said. "That's what he's trying to prove. So please don't drink it for a while."

At the door, I dug into my pocket. I found a halfpenny and handed it to the boy. Henry had been about his age when Pa died.

We had good shoes when Pa was alive, and whenever my feet got too big, Mum would carefully oil the leather on my old shoes and wrap them in brown paper. "Henry, you'll have these to wear to school one day. So eat your porridge up so your feet will grow, grow, grow!"

But after Pa died, there wasn't much money for shoes. At first Mum tried to keep us by doing fine sewing. We had to move from two rooms into one. We sold her pianoforte and all of my father's books. But she still scrimped to send us to school.

I remember she had a little trunk that she kept linen

in, with plain brown sides and a top decorated with yellow tulips and pink roses and purple lavender, painted by hand. I'd always imagined that she'd painted it herself, and I liked to think of her as a girl, making her paintbrush into a tiny point to capture the delicate petals.

One day we came home from school and found her kneeling before the trunk, tears staining her cheeks. She was holding a faded cotton pillowcase.

"See these stitches?" Mum whispered. "I used to be able to make stitches this tiny, almost invisible. But now my eyes have gotten so weak that Mrs. Kingsbury says there are too many mistakes."

After that Mum took to doing laundry for a while. It made her hands red and raw. She cried a lot. And then one day she brought Fisheye Bill Tyler home.

It was evening by the time Dr. Snow and I headed back to Sackville Street. He was frowning and silent as we made our way through the crowds on Regent Street. I thought he was probably worried about not having enough evidence for the committee. He wanted to convince them to take the pump handle off on Thursday. Waiting could mean more deaths.

"No one can predict how long the cholera poison will last," said Dr. Snow. "It may already be disappearing from the water. Or there could be a new contamination any day. We just don't know."

That night, Dr. Snow and I compared notes. It was a

wonder to see how his mind worked. At first I was afraid all my interviews with families would be a jumble. But after looking at my notes and taking stock of his own, Dr. Snow leaned back and tapped his pen on his desk.

"You did well, Eel. I think there can be little doubt that the Broad Street pump is the culprit," he began. "The list you copied at the General Register Office shows us that most of the people who died on Friday and Saturday lived just a short distance from the pump.

"There were only ten deaths in houses near pumps on other streets," he went on. "But five of those families told us they didn't drink water from the pump closest to their house. No, instead they preferred the Broad Street well, and so they always got their water from there."

"What about the other five, sir?" Had we really found out so much?

"Ah, it seems that three were children who went to school near the pump on Broad Street. Their parents think they probably stopped to drink from it," he said. "As for the others, well, they could have drunk the water without even knowing it."

"How could that be?"

"Water from the Broad Street pump is used for mixing with spirits in the Newcastle upon Tyne and other public houses in the neighborhood. And then there's the coffee shop. The woman who runs it told me she sometimes uses water from the pump. She has heard that at least nine of her customers are dead."

That gave me another idea. "What about Italian ice?"

"Italian ice? What about it?"

"There are carts that sell a sweet drink made of a flavored powder and water, what we call Italian ice. I visited a family today who had lost a son," I explained. "They didn't know if he had drunk water from the pump. But I know who he was. I often saw him buying Italian ice. Maybe the water from Broad Street was used to make it."

"Good point." Dr. Snow made a note on his paper.

"Will this be enough for the meeting on Thursday?" I wanted to know.

He looked thoughtful. "I don't think so. Not yet."

Dr. Snow rose and began pacing, his hands clasped behind him. "Everyone in this neighborhood relies on the Broad Street pump. Taking the handle off won't be a popular decision. The committee won't want to do it."

He stopped and shook his head. His shoulders slumped a little, and for a minute he looked beaten.

"Maybe there's something else we can show the committee," I suggested.

"It will have to be something decisive," Dr. Snow replied. "Let me think more about it. Tomorrow we must keep looking."

CHAPTER EIGHTEEN
The Unexpected Case

Wednesday, September 6

Dr. Snow wanted me to be up early. While he breakfasted and worked on his case notes, I cleaned the cages and fed the animals.

I liked working with the small creatures, who had their own tiny wants and troubles. I couldn't help smiling as I watched them, and smiles had been rare since the Great Trouble had come upon us. And when two rabbits began a tug-o'-war over a piece of lettuce, I found myself laughing. I guess it's hard for folks never to laugh, even in the midst of bad times.

Dr. Snow stopped at the shed on his way out. "I'm afraid I can't come to Broad Street this morning. I've got several urgent cases to attend to, including a dentist who needs my help. He has an elderly patient with the stumps of five teeth to extract."

I shuddered. It sounded horrible. "Should I keep knocking on doors and asking questions, Dr. Snow? I haven't finished Berwick Street."

"Yes, lad. Just carry on." Suddenly Dr. Snow slammed his hand on the side of a cage, making the four guinea pigs inside squeal. "I wish we had more time to find the evidence we need."

"We've talked to lots of families who say the people who died drank water from the Broad Street pump," I put in. "I think what we've found should be enough."

"I agree, Eel. But as we discussed last night, changing people's minds isn't easy. This committee is made up of men who are set in their ways. They can see things one way, but not another. They only know the miasma theory," he said.

I'd finished all the cages except for the ones with the guinea pigs. I filled a small bowl with clean water and placed it inside. "I wish I knew what it will take to convince them."

Dr. Snow didn't answer. He was staring intently into the guinea pigs' cage. I followed his gaze. Three guinea pigs had crowded round the fresh water, while one sat in the corner, chewing on a piece of fruit, his little jaws working fast.

"The odd one out," said the doctor softly.

He turned to stare at me, his eyebrows raised, as if I should have understood something from his words. As if they *meant* something.

I looked at the guinea pigs again. At first all I could come up with was that Dr. Snow was a bit daft. That would certainly fit with what Mrs. Weatherburn had told me about the doctor giving himself doses of gas. Maybe the chloroform had gone to his head?

But then I focused on the one guinea pig that was far away from the others. Was that it? *The odd one out.* Guinea pigs around a bowl of water. One in a corner. What was Dr. Snow thinking?

All at once a sound escaped me.

"Have you got it, then, Eel?"

"I . . . I think so. . . . If these here guinea pigs all lived by the pump and drank from it and it had the cholera poison in it, then they'd get sick," I said, my words tumbling out quickly, though I was trying to put it in a scientific sort of way as best I could.

I paused to lick my lips, which were dry from the sun. "But there could be other reasons too—like living close to one another and catchin' it that way, or maybe, like the reverend and other folks say, from the miasma, from bad air on one street. . . ."

"Go on." Dr. Snow folded his arms and watched me.

"Since there could be so many different explanations, it's hard to make a clear case that will convince folks. That's where this other guinea pig comes in—the one over there, all by himself. Suppose he was nowhere near the water. Nowhere near it at all." I spoke slowly, puzzling it out.

"Yet suppose this faraway guinea pig somehow got hold of the water and fell ill," I said. "Maybe someone brought the water to him. But he never got close to the area. And he *never* breathed the same air as the rest of them that died."

"I think you've got it," Dr. Snow urged me on.

"So if we can prove that the *only* thing this here guinea pig has in common with the others that died is that he drank the exact same water, then, it's . . ." I searched for a word. "It's odd. It's unexpected."

"That's precisely it," exclaimed Dr. Snow. "Unexpected. What we need is an unexpected case of cholera."

He pulled his watch out and glanced at the time. "That's our task for tomorrow, when I am free. It could be the last piece of the puzzle."

"Do you think we can find one?"

"Maybe." Dr. Snow picked up his bag and turned to go. "Maybe not. But *if* it does exist and *if* we can find it, history may be made this week."

After Dr. Snow left, I finished up my work and whistled for Dilly. "C'mon, girl. Let's keep investigating. Dr. Snow needs us to find the *unexpected*."

By noon, as I walked up and down the cobblestoned streets—first Broad, then Poland, then Dufours—knocking on doors and asking questions, I hadn't come close to finding an unexpected case of the cholera.

"Maybe Florrie has an idea, Dilly," I said finally. "We haven't seen her since we made the map on Monday afternoon. I need to tell her everything that's happened."

Florrie's older brother, Danny, opened the door to my knocking.

"I thought you was the coffin man," he said in a strange, rough voice. "Mum's gone. We're just waitin' for them to take 'er away."

I stood, a shock of fear running through me. "I'm so sorry, Danny. But . . . what about Florrie? She's all right, isn't she?"

There was a long silence. Danny swallowed hard. "She took sick last night, Eel. We thought it was all over, this epidemic. But I guess not. Poor girl, she don't even know that Mum didn't make it. She nursed Mum all day yesterday and then . . ."

So that was why I hadn't seen Florrie out on the streets yesterday. *I should have come sooner,* I thought.

"Can I see her?"

Danny shook his head. "She wouldn't want it right now," he said. "She's off 'er 'ead part of the time, talking nonsense, slippin' in and out. I heard 'er say your name, Eel."

A sound came from inside.

"I got to go," Danny said. Then he shut the door.

I don't know how long I stood there. Not Florrie. Florrie couldn't have the cholera. I thought of the bucket of water in the corner when she was nursing Bernie. That water had come from the Broad Street pump.

I was still standing on Florrie's doorstep when I saw Gus, the lad we'd met at the Broad Street pump last week. I'd suspected he was sweet on Florrie. I was sure of it now, for he carried a small bouquet of drooping violets.

"How is she, Eel?" Gus wanted to know. "I come by early this morning and Danny told me what happened."

"Not good."

"Do you think . . . it would be all right to knock?"

I shook my head and glanced down at the flowers in his hand. He followed my gaze.

"I know. Pretty sorry-looking," he said ruefully. "I had to buy 'em off a flower seller. I could've picked them meself in Hampstead any day when I took the cart to the Widow Eley's house. But that was before. I don't guess I'll be bringing jugs of water out there anymore. The widow died on Saturday."

I was only half listening to his words at first. And then they hit me. "You mean, you've been taking water from the Broad Street pump out to Hampstead regular-like?"

Gus nodded. "Several times a week at least. Thursday was the last.

"Mrs. Eley's sons at the factory are . . . well, they *were* . . . that devoted to her," Gus went on. "Wanted their mum to have the water she liked, from when she used to live on Broad Street. So that's part of my job. Or it was, anyhow."

I must have been staring at him with my mouth open, because he came close and peered into my face. "You all right, then, Eel?"

I nodded. "I have a question for you. Just where in Hampstead is the Widow Eley's house?"

PART FOUR

The Broad Street Pump

In the "Weekly Return of Births and Deaths" of September 9th, the following death is recorded as occurring in the Hampstead district: "At West End, on 2nd September, the widow of a percussion-cap maker, aged 59 years, diarrhea two hours, cholera epidemics [*sic*] sixteen hours."

I was informed by this lady's son that she had not been in the neighborhood of Broad Street for many months. A cart went from Broad Street to West End every day, and it was the custom to take out a large bottle of the water from the pump in Broad Street, as she preferred it. The water was taken on Thursday, 31st August, and she drank of it in the evening, and also on Friday. She was seized with cholera on the evening of the latter day, and died on Saturday.

—Dr. John Snow,
On the Mode of Communication of Cholera (1855)

CHAPTER NINETEEN
The Widow Eley

I t was several miles to Hampstead. I'd never been so far from home, and I was glad to have Dilly's company. At first I'd been torn about setting out—a part of me wanted to stay near Florrie. But I knew she'd want me to go.

It felt strange to leave the chimneys and coal-dusted buildings behind. Out here, the air had a sweet, earthy scent. It reminded me of wagons on their way to Covent Garden. Whenever they pass by, the stench of the city falls away and you're surrounded by the fresh, fragrant smells of apples, pears, and vegetables.

Only now the smells weren't just from a wagon but from everything around me: sweet, fresh hay in the fields and hedgerows dotted with wild roses. If the blue death was caused by miasma, the way folks believed, I didn't see how anyone in Hampstead could get it.

There were more trees too, with bright green leaves that sparkled in the sunlight. I passed meadows where, like Gus, I might've stopped to pick flowers for Florrie. For every ten steps I took, Dilly ran a hundred—circling back and forth, sniffing under every tree and rock, and now and again chasing a squirrel.

"Maybe you were born some place like this, Dilly," I told her. "If you hadn't gotten lost in Piccadilly Circus when you were a pup, you might be here still."

It wasn't hard to find the right house. I asked a farmer on his way back from bringing produce to town. He pointed it out, saying, "May she rest in peace, poor lady."

Mrs. Susannah Eley had lived in a pretty white cottage, surrounded by a neat fence and a garden bursting with color. I recognized hollyhocks and daisies from seeing them at Covent Garden Market, but there were lots more besides. Bees buzzed everywhere.

I went around to the back and waited till I saw a young housemaid come out with a bucket. She headed to a pump in the backyard. I frowned. Why would Mrs. Eley get water from the Broad Street pump when she had this well? Then I remembered what Gus had said: she had liked the taste of the water from Broad Street best of all.

I knew I couldn't introduce myself as an assistant to Dr. Snow. Any maid who heard that would laugh in my face and scoff, "A great London doctor wouldn't give an urchin like you the time of day."

No, helping the doctor on Broad Street, where folks knew me, was one thing. Here in the country, it was quite another. I'd have to discover what I wanted to know some other way. "Pardon me, miss," I called, taking off my cap. "I'm on my way to my grandpa's house in the center of London. I'm wondering if you could spare a cup of milk."

I smiled and waited for Dilly to charm her. Dilly didn't disappoint. She plopped herself down in front of the little maid, grinned broadly, and swept her tail back and forth on the grass.

"Well, ain't she a sweetie," said the maid. She went inside and brought me out a small tin cup of milk. Then she went back to drawing water.

"Get good water here, do you?" I asked as casually as I could, sipping the milk.

"Well, I've always thought so. But the mistress was partial to the water in her old neighborhood," the maid told me. "Liked it so much her sons had a cart come out every few days with some big jugs of it. I never touched it myself."

"Your mistress, I think, is the Widow Eley, whose sons own a factory on Broad Street?"

"Was. My mistress that was. Poor lady," sighed the

maid. "She got awful sick last week and died on Saturday. Her niece that was visiting from Islington got struck down too."

The girl paused and wiped her face with her apron. She beckoned and I went a little closer. "They say it was the blue death," she whispered. "I had to burn the sheets."

"Have many other folks died of the cholera around here?"

"Oh, no. None whatsoever." The girl looked shocked at the idea. "Just Mrs. Eley and her niece."

"That's very sad," I said. "I expect the two ladies often dined together, with wine and everything?"

"Mrs. Eley never touched wine," she said. "No, I served the two of them water with their dinner on Thursday night. Mrs. Eley always said water was the best thing for a healthy skin and constitution."

Now came the most important question. "And Mrs. Eley's niece . . . she liked the Broad Street water too?"

"Oh, yes! I just left the pitcher on the table, and by the end of dinner it was empty."

So there it was: Mrs. Eley and her niece had both drunk water from the Broad Street pump.

Suddenly the maid began to sniffle. "It's an awful tragedy. The mistress was ever so kind to me. And now . . . I don't know what will happen. I'm just staying on to clean out the house till the family decides."

"I'm sorry, miss," I said. And I was. I knew what it was

like to lose a situation. "I can see that you're a hard worker. I'm sure you'll do well wherever you go."

The girl patted Dilly's head. "Thank you, lad. I hope I shan't have to leave Hampstead. The boy who delivers the water, Gus is his name, tells me such stories about how crowded and dirty a place the center of London is. No, you can keep that."

We talked for a while longer. The maid told me her name was Polly. She was fifteen, just two years older than me. I thought Florrie would like working in a house like this one, with a kind mistress and flowers all about.

If only Florrie could fight off the blue death.

"Dilly," I said on the road heading back, "I think we've found the right clue at last."

For it seemed clear that Gus had brought Mrs. Susannah Eley water from the Broad Street pump several times last week. I'd seen him myself on Monday, the day I'd found Queenie. And now Mrs. Eley and her niece were dead of the cholera.

Polly, who had not drunk the Broad Street water, was perfectly fine. There were no other cases of cholera in the neighborhood. To everyone else, it was a mystery why poor Mrs. Eley got the cholera out here in Hampstead.

But not to me.

Today was Wednesday. If tomorrow night Dr. Snow

could stand up and tell the committee that Mrs. Susannah Eley—far away in a leafy part of Hampstead—had died on Saturday from drinking water from the Broad Street pump, surely they would listen.

I couldn't wait to tell Dr. Snow what I'd found. More than anything, I hoped Florrie would be well enough to hear it too.

CHAPTER TWENTY
Something Else Unexpected

"Let's go, Dilly." I called her back from a meadow. With a swift bark and a grin, Dilly loped after me.

As we walked along, I suddenly made a decision: I needed to track down one last clue. I'd learned that no one who lived near Mrs. Eley had gotten sick. But what about her niece? I should find out if anyone else in *her* neighborhood had been struck with the cholera. It would be, I thought, a final proof.

It was only an extra couple of miles out of my way to Islington. That wasn't much for me. I'd grown up walking across London. Except for the time we took Pa to the burial ground, I'd never ridden in a hansom cab or one of those new horse-drawn omnibuses. (When we buried Mum, we walked, Henry being older then and Fisheye Bill being too stingy to pay for a cab.)

"We'll go," I told Dilly. "And after that we'll stop to see Henry for a few minutes. Henry was so lonely the other day. Besides, he's never met you. You'd better be on your best behavior for Mrs. Miggle. She's like Mrs. Weatherburn—only worse."

I could still do all this and be back at Berwick Street before dark to check on Florrie. And I'd have a lot to tell her—and thank her for too.

For, in a way, it was Florrie who'd led me to the proof we needed. If Gus hadn't come by to visit her that morning, I might never have discovered the unexpected case.

Even without my knowing her name, it didn't take me long to track down Mrs. Eley's niece. All I had to say was "I'm looking for a lady that died of the cholera last week." The second person I asked sent me to a street where one house had a laurel wreath on the door tied up in black crepe and the window shades drawn.

I went to the back and knocked. A sturdy woman dressed in mourning black opened the door.

"Excuse me, but today I saw Polly, who works in Mrs. Eley's house," I began, pulling off my cap. "She mentioned your recent trouble. I thought you might have some messages to be run."

"You're too late, lad," the servant answered. "The mistress was buried yesterday. We sent the funeral notices out by post, though we could have used help to deliver some by hand."

"I'm sorry, ma'am," I replied. "Did your mistress get struck down the same as Mrs. Eley, then?"

She nodded. "And I don't mind telling you that the rest of us in the household feared for our lives. Mistress went away on Thursday night to take dinner with her aunt, as healthy as could be. She come back Friday and took sick."

She sniffed noisily. "By Saturday afternoon, bless her sweet soul, she was lying in a coffin. She leaves two boys, younger than you."

"I'm sorry to hear it," I said. I took a breath. Now for the question that mattered. "Can you tell me, has the cholera afflicted anyone else in this neighborhood?"

I waited for her answer, my heart beating hard. But I wasn't surprised when I heard it.

"Oh, dear, no. This is a healthy part of Islington. Why, I don't know that I've ever heard of the cholera being in these streets, at least in my time," she replied, dabbing her cheeks with her handkerchief.

She stopped to blow her nose. "No, it is a tragic mystery indeed that both aunt and niece were carried off in this way. I don't suppose we will ever know why."

I thanked her and left. The woman was wrong, I

thought. *We know exactly why they died. They both drank water from the Broad Street pump.*

I walked quickly toward Mrs. Miggle's lodging house, which sat on the edge of a crowded neighborhood. I'd given Henry strict instructions to always walk straight home from school and not wander around.

"Make yourself invisible," I'd told him many times. "Fisheye Bill Tyler favors workin' in the Borough or the Seven Dials, and criminals like to keep to their own territories. So I don't expect him to be snooping around here. Still, you can't be too careful."

But forgetting that was exactly the mistake I made that sunny afternoon. I was eager to boast to my little brother about my new job helping a great doctor. I was already thinking ahead to telling Florrie about solving the mystery.

In short, I was so full of myself I forgot to be cautious. I forgot about Fisheye Bill. But he hadn't forgotten me. He was like an octopus, his long tentacles reaching out over the hidden nooks and crannies of London.

When I heard the clop of hooves stop close behind me, I didn't turn around. There were cabs everywhere on the streets. Then came the sound of footsteps behind me. But I didn't notice in time.

Instead I was deep into imagining the moment of triumph Dr. Snow and I would have before the committee. Would he, I wondered, call on me to give the evidence

I'd found today? No, that would be too much to ask. But he might at least turn and smile at me. That would be enough.

One minute the hazy yellow sky was ahead of me. The next I was clawing at my face, trying to breathe under a foul-smelling hand. I bit down hard and kicked and flailed. But I was picked up and carried back to the cab, then thrown inside like a sack of onions.

Suddenly I realized I knew the smell that enveloped me. It was the smell of fish.

And that was the last thought I had before something knocked into my head so hard everything went black.

I awoke to a rocky to-and-fro motion that made my stomach lurch. It took me a minute to piece together fragments of what I was feeling—a pounding in my head, the rocking motion of a horse, a cord digging into my wrists, a kerchief over my eyes—and, most of all, the smell.

Slowly my brain linked one sensation to the next and then the next. It was a bit like a piecework quilt I'd once watched my mum put together. The pattern didn't make sense right away, not until you could see all the pieces.

Finally I figured it out: I was in a hansom cab, pulled by a single horse clop-clopping over the cobblestones, on my way to who knew where. I had been spotted and grabbed the one time when my guard was down.

I had been kidnapped by my stepfather.

How had this happened? Fisheye Bill couldn't have been following me. It was just a horrible coincidence. I cursed my bad luck. At least I could be grateful that he'd picked me up before I'd gotten to Mrs. Miggle's lodging house.

Though what Fisheye Bill was doing riding in a cab like a swell was beyond me. *He must've just done a job,* I thought. Housebreaking, perhaps, in some nice Islington neighborhood. And then, all out of the blue, he'd been given a present: me.

Now, as we bumped along, I tried to get my bearings. It would help to know where he was taking me. I concentrated hard, hoping to catch a familiar sound—a church bell, a boat on the Thames, the crush of traffic at Piccadilly Circus.

Then I remembered Dilly. She must be wandering alone, scared and confused. This city was a cruel place for a dog. Dilly, like so many of my friends on Broad Street this past week, was probably lost for good.

After a while the cab stopped and the door opened.

"Don't play dead, boy," came Fisheye's voice out of the thick heat. "I can tell you're awake. Now look sharp. We have some catching up to do. Get down."

I didn't move. Suddenly I felt a sharp kick in my ribs. "Ow!"

Fisheye pulled me down from the cab and dragged me along for a few steps. I heard a door open and he pushed me forward.

"Walk up them stairs," he ordered. "I ain't carrying you." I stumbled up, best I could. The stairwell smelled like a sewer.

At the top he pushed me into a dank room and threw me into a chair. "Don't move."

He reached around and took the blindfold off.

"Where are we?" I asked.

Fisheye just laughed. "You're home, Eel. Home with your daddy."

I frowned. This dirty room could be anywhere.

I should have been able to tell if the cab had crossed into Southwark over the Thames. I would've smelled the oily brown river when we passed over. I would've heard the boats. Or had that happened when I was knocked out cold? I didn't know.

I felt dizzy, and like I might be sick. But I couldn't let that stop me. I had to pay more attention now. No matter what happened or how much my head hurt.

"I won't tell you anything," I said. "Why can't you just leave me alone? I'm nothing to you."

"Oh, my dear boy, you surprise me," said Fisheye. "What kind of stepfather would I be to leave two young boys to fend for themselves in London, crawlin' as it is with criminals and thieves?"

"I'm just trouble to you," I pointed out. "I won't steal for you. I'll just run away again. Or worse, I'll turn you in."

He laughed. "I doubt that. But you see, lad, it's not you I want."

I clenched my fists and half rose in the chair.

"Yes, you know exactly what I mean, don't you?" Fisheye smirked. "I want your little brother. Because what brings in more tin than a small, delicate boy with great, round eyes?

"He takes after your dearly departed mum, don't 'e?" Fisheye went on. "Henry don't look at all like the usual street urchin. No, he's what you might call adorable. Just the sort of boy to soften a lady's heart . . . and make her open her purse."

Begging. He wanted to turn Henry into a beggar. And when the takings were slow, he'd want him to be a pick-pocket too.

"So tell me, Eel," growled Fisheye. "Where have you got 'im stashed?"

He paused and blew his foul breath into my face. "Where is Henry?"

CHAPTER TWENTY-ONE
In Which I Am Held Prisoner

Fisheye badgered me for most of that long, awful afternoon. But I wouldn't give in. He was still at it when I heard the downstairs door open and heels clop up the creaky stairs. In a minute the room was flooded with a sickly sweet perfume, strong enough to make me gag.

"Well, well. What you got here, Bill?"

"This 'ere's my stepson, Kate. The one I told you about from my married days, short and sweet as they were," Fisheye Bill told a thin, sharp-looking woman.

She had bright spots of red on her cheeks, and even redder lips. She smiled, showing yellow teeth stained with brown streaks. "Got 'im at last, eh, Bill?"

The woman came close and stuck her face right into

mine. I was almost overtaken by the smells: beer and fish and tobacco, all mixed with that stinky perfume.

"But 'e ain't pretty, except for the saucer eyes on 'im," she said in surprise. "I thought you said 'e would make our fortune."

"Not this one, Kate," Fisheye Bill growled. "This 'ere boy is the big one. 'E's got the little one hidden from me."

Kate put her hands on her hips and looked at me in mock astonishment. "Well, I never. Who ever heard of such a thing? Hidin' a child from his own devoted father. That's a cruel thing for a lad to do. Dangerous too."

"Cruel and dangerous," agreed Fisheye Bill. "And now that you're home, love, you can hold 'im down so I can take the strap to him, like any good father would when 'is son goes against his wishes."

"Before I've had me tea?" Kate shook her head, and a thin strand of oily hair escaped her cap. "'Ave a heart, Bill. I been workin' all day."

Working? I couldn't imagine what kind of work Kate did. *Probably another thief,* I thought. I glanced down at the floorboards, which were black with grime and splotches of grease.

I thought of how Abel Cooper had taught me to keep the floors of the Lion Brewery clean. "As clean as if you might drink ale right off 'em," he'd said.

I'd been wrong. Even if I'd been too cowardly to talk to Mr. Edward, I should have gone back to see Abel Cooper.

Maybe, like Florrie, he was a friend, one I could have trusted with my secret—and the whole truth about Henry and me.

But I hadn't done that. Instead I had got myself into trouble. Great trouble indeed.

I wish I could say that after a good amount of gin, Fisheye and Kate forgot about me and I escaped. But that's not what happened. In fact, eating a hot steak-and-kidney pie seemed to give Fisheye extra energy for the strap, which he used on me with considerable force, with Kate holding me down.

I can say, though, that maybe I cried, and maybe I yelled, and I might've even used some words that my mum told me not to say—but I never told where Henry was.

After a while Fisheye threw the strap down in disgust. "I'm off to the pub. This vile creature has worn me out. We'll see what he says in the morning after no supper and no breakfast. I expect he'll change his tune."

"You ain't gonna leave me alone w'im, are you, Bill?" asked Kate, rubbing her thin hands together nervously. "What if 'e gets loose and turns on me?"

"I'll tie him down under the iron bedstead," Fisheye said. "He can lie on the floor and call it a good bed. Can't you, boy?"

"Better gag him, just the same," Kate suggested.

Fisheye stuffed an old, smelly rag in my mouth and tied it tight. After he left, Kate stretched out on the bed above me and was soon snoring up a storm. My mouth felt dry and sore. The welts on my back stung something fierce.

I tried to come up with some way to escape. It was no use. It might've been the effects of being beaten, or the long walk in the sun, but a dark wave came over me and there was nothing I could do. I slept.

CHAPTER TWENTY-TWO
Things Look Grim

Thursday, September 7

I woke to loud snores and a burning need to use the chamber pot. My lips under the rag were cracked and dried. My jaw ached. I was hungry but queasy at the same time. I was used to being up early to work. But I doubted that Fisheye Bill and Kate ever rolled out of bed before midmorning.

I tried feebly to get their attention, banging my heels against the floor. My yells came out like low growls. Suddenly there was a knock on the door. Fisheye Bill grunted, half asleep, "What?"

It opened. Even if I hadn't seen him with my own eyes, I would've smelled him: Nasty Ned.

"Got some coal to sell you and the missus, Bill," he

began. All at once he spotted me lying tied up under the bed. His eyes closed to slits. He cleared his throat. "Thrup-penceworth today."

Fisheye Bill hauled himself out of bed and put some coins in Ned's hand. Then he grabbed Ned's wrist so hard the mudlark cried out. "Eeow! What you wanna do that for?"

"I see you've noticed that young Eel is here for a visit," Fisheye Bill said smoothly. "And I thank you for telling me that my dear stepson was still in town. But I don't want a word of this to anyone, hear me?"

Ned gulped and stared right at me with large, fright-ened eyes. "I didn't think he was goin' to torture you, Eel. I didn't think that!"

"Don't talk to him!" Fisheye yelled, raising his hand toward Ned.

Ned flinched but didn't take a step back. "You're not gonna kill 'im, are you, Fisheye?"

"No, I ain't. But I'll tell you what's to happen. You done me a good deed, and I did one for you: I bought your coal for an extra good price," Fisheye Bill declared. "But that's the end of it. Like I said, you better keep your mouth shut about this. This is my private matter. A private *family* matter."

Fisheye drew out the word, *fam-i-leee,* and smirked as he said it.

Ned moved his bare feet nervously on the floor, his toes almost black with mud. "I ain't seen nothin', Fisheye. I'll be off now. Good day to you."

Ned closed the door, then clattered down the stairs and was gone. Nasty Ned. I should have known. It had been Ned who'd let on to Fisheye Bill that I wasn't dead.

It was probably good that I was tied up. Because otherwise, I might have rushed at Ned and done something my mother wouldn't have approved of at all.

When Ned had gone, Fisheye allowed me to use the chamber pot and gave me a sip of water.

"Now, Kate and me, we got a little business to do that can't be put off," he told me. "A little breakfast and a little business. Then, when I get back, you and me are going to visit Henry. You got that, boy?"

I clammed up. I wasn't about to answer him. But when they'd left me alone in the hot, close room, I began to think.

Things looked grim on all accounts. First there was Florrie. I couldn't bear her thinking I'd forgotten her. Then Dilly. She was probably already lost. Despite what Mr. Griggs had said about her sense of direction, I didn't expect she'd be able to find her way to Dr. Snow's house.

Finally, there was Dr. Snow. Tonight was the committee meeting. If I didn't get there in time, he wouldn't have the information about the unexpected case of Mrs. Susannah Eley, which proved that the water from the Broad Street pump had caused the cholera outbreak.

Without that proof, the chances that the committee would agree to remove the pump handle weren't so good.

And that, I knew, meant more people might die.

I suddenly remembered Dr. Snow's face on that first day at the pump. I'd wanted him to rush up and save Bernie. But he couldn't—I realized that now.

What Dr. Snow wanted was to unlock the mystery of the blue death—not just for the victims of this outbreak, but for everyone in the future. Taking the handle off the Broad Street pump would just be the beginning—the start of a time when innocent people like Bernie and his parents wouldn't have to die from a disease they didn't understand. So that bright girls like Florrie wouldn't have to suffer.

What was my life, or Henry's life, against all those future lives that could be saved? Should I trade my freedom for Henry's?

My head hurt just thinking about it. I didn't know the right thing to do. All I knew was that Henry was my little brother. I'd promised Mum to protect him. That was my job in life, more or less. How could I betray him?

No matter how I looked at it, everything seemed lost.

Time is a strange thing. On the river, I could tell what time it was from the tide and the light. Sometimes I could hear the great bells of St. Paul's Cathedral chime the hours. I'd heard church bells here, but what with my head hurting and my dozing off now and again, I couldn't be sure what time it was. I began to wonder if Fisheye Bill and Kate would ever get back.

But then came the moment when I heard another new sound. I was curled on my side on the filthy floor. I ached all over. I raised my head a little, leastwise as much as I could, still being under the bed.

Clump, clump. Clump, clump.

Someone was coming up the wooden stairs. Fisheye must be back. My heart sank. I still didn't have a plan.

I tensed, listening. The steps halted in front of the door. The silence lengthened. It was almost as if the person on the other side was listening. Suddenly the door flew open, slamming against the wall.

Thumbless Jake filled the doorway like a giant creature come out of the river.

"Jake!" I croaked, though of course it didn't sound like that with the rag in my mouth.

He looked down at me and shook his great head. "Always in trouble."

Thumbless Jake came closer. Then I noticed.

In his good hand he had a small, shiny knife. I gulped. Was he going to do me in? Then Jake flashed a queer sort of smile.

"Now, what did I tell you, lad? We're all riverfinders," he said, bending down to cut the rope that bound me. "And today it looks like you're the bit o' something shiny that it's my lot to find."

CHAPTER TWENTY-THREE
The Decision

As it turned out, Ned had been so frightened that Bill would kill me and he'd be haunted by my ghost, he'd run and found Thumbless Jake and told him the whole story.

"He got a good shaking from me, I'll tell you," said Jake after he'd helped me down the rickety steps.

"Where are we?" I asked, rubbing my hands where the rope had been.

"Down in the Borough," Jake answered. "Somewhere near Lant Street."

"Lant Street!" I exclaimed. We were probably two miles from Broad Street. "What time is it?"

I could tell from the shadows on the street that it was early evening already. I'd slept a lot longer than I thought.

Lucky for me, Fisheye and Kate had gotten delayed somewhere, doing some sort of criminal activity. Or, just as likely, they'd gotten drunk in a pub and lost track of the hours.

But if it was late, that meant I didn't have much time to get to the committee meeting, which would begin at seven o'clock. As if in answer, Jake's stomach rumbled.

"Time? It's time for my tea." He grinned. "I should think it's after six. Not, mind you, that I pay much attention to the hours these days. I mostly just flow with the tides."

After six! We began walking toward Borough Road. From there, I figured, I could make my way to Waterloo Bridge and then north to Soho.

All at once, a woman rushed up to me and grabbed my arm. I yelled and pulled away, thinking it was Kate.

"It *is* you!" the woman exclaimed. A small girl came running up behind her. "It's him, Betsy! It's that boy from Broad Street."

"Betsy!" I cried.

Betsy threw her arms around me. "Eel, you came! Just like you said you would. But where's Dilly?"

I couldn't answer because suddenly Betsy's aunt was grabbing my hands and talking at great speed into my face. "I am that glad to see you, dear lad. You must think me a perfect witch after how I acted the other day. I've always been this way, flying off the handle and saying things I don't mean. Just the opposite of my dear brother, who was as mellow as an old mare. I'm right sorry."

She pulled Betsy close to her. "Perhaps it was the grief and shock that got hold o' me. Betsy is a dear girl, and my husband and I are lucky to have her."

I was happy for Betsy's sake. But time was short. Fisheye Bill could appear at any minute. And I had to get over the river and all the way to Soho soon. Very soon.

And then I had an inspiration.

"Ma'am, I believe you mentioned that your husband kept a cab," I said urgently. "By any chance . . . would your husband—and his horse—be home now?"

Betsy's aunt had just opened her mouth to answer when something fast and strong slammed into me and knocked me down, making wild grunting noises. Chaos erupted.

"Now, what's this?" I heard Jake say.

"You did bring Dilly," cried Betsy, clapping her hands. "You brought her, after all!"

It was quite late Thursday evening by the time I got to Berwick Street, eager to tell Florrie the whole incredible story. And the most incredible thing of all was that she was alive to hear it.

Florrie was lying in a small bed. I pulled a chair up beside her. I'd never been to the Bakers' rooms before. Florrie shared one with her sister, Nancy, a special luxury for our neighborhood.

On the walls around her bed hung sketches she had

done. I recognized our friends and neighbors: Annie Ribbons holding a sewing basket that overflowed with thread, bits of lace, and streams of ribbons. Mrs. Lewis with baby Fanny in her arms. Mr. Griggs cutting cloth for a new jacket. And there were Betsy and Bernie, who was throwing a stick for Dilly, all three of them smiling. There was even a picture of me and my mudlark bag, with Little Queenie's head poking out.

Florrie's father had let me in and warned that I couldn't stay long. "She's holding her own and resting comfortable-like," he told me. "But don't tire her out, lad. I've lost my wife and can't bear the thought of losing my dear girl too."

"She's strong, Mr. Baker," I told him. "She'll make it."

Florrie's face was as white as paper, but her skin didn't have that awful blue tinge I'd seen on Mr. Griggs and Bernie. That gave me real hope.

"Hullo, Eel. Sorry I missed you yesterday," she said weakly, holding out her hand to me. "I missed a lot this week, once Mum took sick. . . ."

Her voice trailed off and she began to cry.

"I'm so sorry, Florrie." I squeezed her hand gently.

After a while Florrie said, "It's Thursday, ain't it? You know, all the time I was sick, I kept thinking that even if I died, you'd be helping Dr. Snow."

Her eyes looked enormous in her thin face. "And did you, Eel? Did you and Dr. Snow solve the mystery?"

"We did. But it's a long story. It starts even before I knew you," I said.

"Tell me everything!"

I told Florrie about meeting Gus on her doorstep, and how he'd given me the clue to the unexpected case. I told her about going to Hampstead with Dilly to track down the story of the Widow Eley. I explained about Islington too, and how Mrs. Eley's niece had been the only case of cholera in her neighborhood.

Then I let on about Henry, and how I'd been keeping him secret all these months. And that led to telling Florrie how Fisheye Bill Tyler had snatched me, and how everything seemed lost until Thumbless Jake rescued me. Finally I got to the part where we'd met Betsy and her aunt near Lant Street, and how Mr. Griggs had been right all along about Dilly. She did have a good sense of direction.

"What happened then?" Florrie wanted to know. "What about tonight? Tell me!"

And so I did.

We had all piled into the cab together—me and Betsy and Dilly, Thumbless Jake, and even Betsy's aunt, whose name turned out to be Mrs. Edith Flanders.

The cab rocked so hard that Dilly got scared and began whining and trying to sit on my lap. Her nails scraped my legs. Betsy giggled, which set off Thumbless Jake, who made a great huffing sound. I'd never heard him laugh before.

Mr. Flanders, the cabbie, was known as Figgie— leastwise that's what Betsy's aunt called him. He drove his horse wildly across Waterloo Bridge. Betsy's aunt kept hollering out the cab window, "Faster, Figgie! You can do it!"

This last part made Florrie's eyes sparkle.

"Somehow we arrived without tipping over," I said. "Dr. Snow was standing in front of a table with several men sitting there. That was the board of governors. I didn't know any of 'em from the neighborhood. But they sure seemed old and dignified, with white hair and whiskers and solemn expressions.

"First thing I heard when I come in was Dr. Snow talking in that strange, husky voice he has. He had our map out, and I expect he was goin' on about 'the mode of communication of cholera' and suchlike."

I explained how we'd added a little mark on the map for each person who died, and how it was clear that those marks were all clustered round the Broad Street pump, and how this showed that the water—not the air—was the cause of the disease.

"Did they believe him, Eel?" Florrie whispered.

I shook my head. "No, they did not. I could tell from their questions they weren't convinced. Leastwise not convinced enough to cause disruption to the neighborhood by taking away one of folks' favorite sources of water."

"So what did you do?"

"I was in the doorway, on account of I'd leaped from the cab and come in first. And I was just listening quietly when suddenly everyone else burst in behind me: Betsy, and her uncle and aunt, and Dilly, and Thumbless Jake from the river." I laughed at the memory of it and held my nose. "You can imagine that Jake sure got everyone's attention. Every head turned to look at us.

"'What's the meaning of this?' demanded the gentleman in charge.

"I could tell that Dr. Snow was too shocked to say a word. And so was Reverend Whitehead, who was there too. So it was up to me," I told Florrie.

"Dilly and I strode right up to stand beside Dr. Snow. 'I'm Dr. Snow's assistant,' I announced. 'I'm called Eel. And Piccadilly, that's my dog here, she and I have tracked down an unexpected case that will prove Dr. Snow's theory. And if you will bear with me, sirs, I believe we can convince you to take the handle off the Broad Street pump so no more people get sick.'"

"My goodness, you must've sounded like a gentleman's son!" Florrie clapped her hands in delight. "What did they say then?"

"You could've heard a pin drop, it was that quiet. One of the men on the committee turned to Dr. Snow and said, very gruff and annoyed, 'Dr. Snow, is what this urchin says true? Are you making a mockery of our proceedings?'

"'No, sir, not at all. I suggest we listen to this boy's report,' Dr. Snow replied, all calm. 'I, for one, am eager to hear it.'

"So I told them how I'd learned yesterday morning that a widow from Hampstead named Susannah Eley had been getting water from the Broad Street pump every day.

"'A boy named Gus from the Eley Brothers factory would take it to her in a little cart several times a week,' I testified. 'I myself witnessed him drawing that water on the morning of Monday, August 28, from the Broad Street pump.'"

"That's right," exclaimed Florrie. "We were there, weren't we? It was the day you found Queenie."

"Yes, and so when I saw Gus on your doorstep yesterday, I remembered that. And then he told me the woman had died last Saturday from the cholera," I explained.

"Go on, then. What happened next?"

I laughed. "Well, at that point Thumbless Jake starts making a ruckus in the back of the room, jabbing Betsy's uncle in the ribs.

"'Will you listen to that boy?' he boomed. 'Used to be a mudlark, he did. But I helped give him a new start in life. And now he sounds as grand as a doctor himself.'"

Florrie was laughing so hard tears streamed down her cheeks. "Go on."

"By this time the committee chair was red in the face. He jumps up, yelling, 'Order! Order in this meeting, please!'

"But then Dr. Snow starts talking too, all excited

because he's so eager to hear about the unexpected case I found. 'Please, gentlemen! Let the boy speak.' And he motions for me to keep talking."

I paused to take a breath. "Here, Florrie, I'll pretend I'm giving the speech all over again."

I stood up and gave a little bow. "This is what I said:

"'I am sorry for the interruption, sir. But when I heard about the Widow Eley, I decided to investigate for myself. I walked to Hampstead with Dilly here, and I found out that Susannah Eley had indeed died from cholera after drinking the water Gus brought her from the Broad Street pump.

"'Not only that, she was the only death from cholera in the neighborhood, which I think Dr. Snow will be able to confirm with the General Register Office.'"

I stopped to take a breath. Florrie nodded for me to keep talking.

"'And that's not all. I found out from a servant in Mrs. Eley's house that her niece had been visiting and had also drunk the water. So after leaving Hampstead, I walked to the neighborhood of Islington. I found the niece's house and confirmed that, once again, this death from cholera was the only one in the neighborhood.

"'I believe, sirs, that this evidence supports Dr. Snow's theory that cholera is spread by water—in this case, water from the Broad Street pump. And I hope you will agree to his request to remove the handle to protect the people of Golden Square, so that no more of my friends and neighbors will die.'"

I stopped, out of breath, just as I had been at the meeting. "I never made such a long speech in my life, Florrie. I tell you that by the time I was done, my legs were shaking. It was a good thing Dr. Snow came over and put his arm around my shoulders, or else I might have collapsed right there."

"And did they believe you?" Florrie asked. "Are they going to take the handle off?"

"It will happen tomorrow morning at ten," I told her. "If you are better, Danny and I will carry you down the street to see it happen. And before you know it, we'll be sittin' in the sun, eating hard-boiled eggs.

"Mrs. Gaskell has a new novel, called *North and South,* which will come out a bit at a time in the *Household Words* magazine. I hear it's got a girl heroine in it—someone brave like you. We can read it together."

"I'm not brave at all. I'm still awful scared," Florrie admitted.

"You're gonna make it," I promised her. "Tell me you believe it."

"I do. I believe we'll soon be sittin' in the sunshine, reading and eating hard-boiled eggs."

Florrie's father came to the doorway and cleared his throat. "It's time, son. Let her rest."

"I'll come back in the morning."

"I'll be here waiting."

And then I leaned over and touched her forehead with a kiss.

CHAPTER TWENTY-FOUR
The Handle

Friday, September 8

"**R**emember this day, lad," said Dr. Snow as we pushed our way through the crowds on Regent Street the next morning. I could hear the excitement in his voice.

"Today we are using science—not superstition—to stop the spread of disease. You and I may not live to see the day, and my name may be forgotten when it comes, but the time will arrive when great outbreaks of cholera will be things of the past," he declared. "And it is the knowledge of the way in which the disease is propagated which will cause them to disappear."

I didn't say anything for a while. I was too busy repeating his words to myself so I could remember them always.

When we got near Broad Street, I asked, "Dr. Snow, do I have time to stop by Florrie's house to look in on her?"

Dr. Snow waved a hand. "Don't be late."

Danny came to the door. For a minute I stood frozen, afraid.

"Don't look like that," I cried.

"She took a turn for the worse around midnight." He rubbed his eyes. Had he been crying? "I don't mind telling you we were all scared."

"And now?" I said urgently. "Is Florrie all right now?"

"Yes, she's much better. Drank a lot of water, which seemed to help. Not from the Broad Street pump, of course. Said she was starting to feel like herself again."

"Then why are you rubbing your eyes?" I demanded, wanting to shake him. "Why do you look so awful?"

"Sleeping," he muttered. "All of us were sleeping for the first time in days when you come along and started banging on the door. You woke me up. Go away, Eel. Come back later."

He was just about to close the door when he stopped. "Oh, wait a minute. Florrie made something for you."

He disappeared for a moment, then returned, holding out a sheet of paper.

"She did it after you left last night, when she wasn't sure if she'd make it or not. Made me promise to give it to you.

She said today is special or something and that you'd know what she means."

"I do know," I said, taking the paper.

It was a simple pencil sketch. Florrie had drawn the Broad Street pump. She had drawn it without the handle. And on the bottom she had scribbled the date: *September 8, 1854.*

Danny yawned and disappeared inside.

I stood on the doorstep with the sketch in my hand and laughed out loud.

"Did you hear that, Dilly? Florrie's getting better!"

I looked around the small crowd. Dr. Snow had worked so hard for this moment. I had too. Florrie believed in what we were doing. Hundreds of people had died already because of the water from this pump. But the folks standing around us that day weren't convinced.

"This 'ere water is a far sight cleaner than the disgusting liquid in the cistern by my house," said one man behind me.

Another called out, "Who come up with this crazy idea? There ain't nothin' wrong with the Broad Street pump. It's the bad air makin' us sick. Can't the committee do something about that?"

I searched for familiar faces—and to my surprise, I saw Mr. Edward Huggins and Abel Cooper standing together in the back of the crowd. I gulped. Mr. Edward caught my eye and beckoned me over to him.

"My brother told me he dismissed you for stealing last week, young man," he said sternly. "I must say I am very disappointed."

"I didn't steal anything, Mr. Huggins," I said, raising my chin to look him in the eyes. "But . . . I couldn't get Mr. Griggs to vouch for me, on account of he got sick."

"You didn't bother coming back to defend yourself, though, did you?" Abel Cooper put in. "You just up and took off, and left me with that cat."

I took a deep breath. I'd made up my mind to tell them the truth, but now that the time had come, it was harder than I expected.

"I'm sorry, Mr. Cooper. And I apologize to you, Mr. Huggins," I said. "I was scared. And . . . I thought it wouldn't do any good, especially once I knew Mr. Griggs wouldn't be able to speak up for me. I figured it would just be Hugz—uh, Herbert's word against mine."

"So you assumed I too would think you guilty?" Mr. Edward asked.

"But—but don't you, sir?" I stammered.

"That depends, lad, on what account you have to give of yourself." Mr. Edward nodded toward Dr. Snow. "You may not have seen me, but I've watched you this week from my office."

I gulped and stared down at my feet, afraid of what he might say next.

"Look at me, lad."

My head shot up.

"I saw you helping families and the coffin man. I saw you walking the streets with Dr. Snow. I was even there in the back at the committee meeting," said Mr. Edward. He chuckled and shook his head. "Now that's something I'll not soon forget—smell and all."

I noticed that the corner of his mouth was twitching. Mr. Edward, I realized, was trying not to laugh.

"So, Eel, when this is over, come see me. I don't know that I can get you your situation back," he said. "My older brother is a stubborn man, and I'm not sure I want to subject a good-hearted lad like you to the companionship of my nephew again. But perhaps I can help you in some way."

"Thank you, sir," I said. "Thank you very much, Mr. Huggins."

Abel Cooper clapped me on the back, a wide grin on his face. "But don't get any ideas of taking your cat back, son. Queenie is my girl now."

PART FIVE

The Last Death
and the First Case

Care should be taken that the water employed for drinking and preparing food (whether it come from a pump-well, or be conveyed in pipes) is not contaminated with the contents of cesspools, house-drains, or sewers; or, in the event that water free from suspicion cannot be obtained, it should be well boiled, and, if possible, also filtered.

–Dr. John Snow,
On the Mode of Communication of Cholera (1855)

CHAPTER TWENTY-FIVE
In Which the Mystery Is Solved

After that day, into the next week, though we kept asking questions of families who had lost someone, it seemed we were coming across fewer new cases of cholera. I mentioned it to Dr. Snow.

"That could very well be, Eel."

"Does that mean . . . taking the pump handle off is working already?"

"Well, probably the epidemic would have been winding down by now anyway, unless there had been a new source of contamination in the water," Dr. Snow explained. "But the pump handle may have saved some lives."

He sighed. "It would have saved more if we could have done it even earlier."

There was still a lot we didn't know. Like how the water got contaminated with the cholera poison in the first place.

"We may never know," said Dr. Snow one evening in his study. "And we may never find the index case either."

"The index case?" asked Rev. Whitehead.

Yes, the reverend was there. For that was something else that had changed.

Rev. Whitehead and Dr. Snow had begun to work together. Both had been asked to be part of the St. James Cholera Inquiry Committee, which was formally investigating the epidemic. And as Rev. Whitehead had talked to the families and listened more closely to Dr. Snow's ideas, he began to change his mind about the doctor's theory. Soon he was one of Dr. Snow's strongest advocates.

"The index case is the first case," Dr. Snow was saying.

"But wasn't that Mr. Griggs?" I asked from where I sat by the fire, with Dilly at my feet. The nights were cooler now, and Mrs. Weatherburn was letting me sleep on a cot in a corner of the kitchen. "At least until your future is settled," she had said.

Dr. Snow shook his head. "It might seem that Mr. Griggs was the index case, because he was the first person we know of who got sick and died. But we have to look further to find a case that explains how the water in the Broad Street well got poisoned with cholera. Other people died during those first three days—seventy-nine on Friday and Saturday alone. They likely contracted the disease at about the same time as Mr. Griggs did. And they became sick because somehow the poison that causes cholera seeped into the well."

"So someone else got sick first and somehow the water became contaminated," Rev. Whitehead said thoughtfully. "But we just haven't found out who it was—or how that happened."

Annie's father, Constable Thomas Lewis, was the last victim of the epidemic. He died on Tuesday, September 19.

I went to see Mrs. Lewis soon after, to pay my respects and bring some fresh eggs and embroidery thread that I'd got from Mrs. Weatherburn for Annie Ribbons. I also wanted to invite Annie to come with Florrie and me to see Dr. Snow's menagerie again.

"You do like animals, don't you? Weren't you carrying some kind of creature squirming in your bag when I saw you at the pump a while back?" Mrs. Lewis asked. "I was so frantic that morning I didn't ask you about it properly."

"It was a cat. She still lives at the Lion." I grinned. "The foreman, Mr. Cooper, is quite attached to her now."

I thought back to the morning I found Little Queenie, when Gus had waited his turn so that he could load up a jug to bring to Mrs. Susannah Eley in Hampstead.

"Mrs. Lewis," I asked suddenly, "Fanny was sick that day, wasn't she? I remember you telling me that."

"Yes, poor little dear," she replied with a sigh. "She lasted until that Saturday. Dr. Rogers said she had just gotten so weak from diarrhea her little body couldn't recover."

"But Dr. Rogers didn't think she had the cholera?" I asked, my mind racing with possibilities.

"No, he didn't think so. After all, Fanny was sick that last Monday morning of August," said Mrs. Lewis. "She was sick before anyone else, before the Great Trouble began."

Before anyone else. Fanny had been sick three days before Mr. Griggs became ill. *What if Dr. Rogers had been wrong?*

I ran to find Florrie, and together we tracked down Rev. Whitehead.

That night, all of us gathered in Dr. Snow's study. Dr. Snow and Rev. Whitehead listened to me for a long time.

A few days later, the St. James Cholera Inquiry Committee gathered in the cellar of 40 Broad Street to interview Mrs. Lewis. She told them that she had soaked Fanny's diapers in buckets all during the week of the baby's illness. Then she had dumped the soiled water out into the cesspool.

The committee brought in Mr. York, a surveyor, to excavate the cesspool and the waste pipe that connected it to the sewer. Mr. York found that the walls of the cesspool were lined with bricks—*decaying* bricks. He discovered that between the cesspool and the Broad Street well, there was a lot of swampy soil, full of human waste. He also found that the well was only two feet and eight inches from the cesspool.

And so, what had happened was this:

The Broad Street well had been contaminated by water and sewage seeping into its walls from the cellar of 40 Broad Street, where Mrs. Lewis had been soaking Fanny's diapers.

The death certificate for Fanny Lewis said that she died of exhaustion after an attack of diarrhea. But that wasn't the full story.

"Fanny Lewis was the first case, what we call the index case," said Dr. Snow. "We will never know how she got it. But now we know that the cholera poison in her diapers seeped into the well, contaminating the water from the Broad Street pump."

Fanny had died of cholera. Cholera that had then killed 615 other people.

"Dr. Snow, Fanny died on Saturday, a week before they took the pump handle off," I said, trying to work out the puzzle. "Is her death why the epidemic started to slow down the second week?"

"Yes, most likely. We're not sure how long the cholera poison stays active, but Mrs. Lewis was no longer washing out Fanny's diapers in the cesspool after Saturday, September second," Dr. Snow explained. "So the outbreak was probably nearing its end by September eighth, when the pump handle came off. Fewer new cases were occurring because the cholera poison was gone from the water, although, of course, people might still have been drinking contaminated water from the well that they had stored in their homes."

Florrie spoke up. "But what about Fanny's father? Didn't he get sick too?"

Dr. Snow nodded. "Constable Lewis was struck with cholera very late in the epidemic, on the afternoon of September eighth, the very day the pump handle was removed."

I tried to piece out what that meant. "So, if Mrs. Lewis emptied buckets of her husband's waste into her cesspool in the cellar, just as she had done with Fanny's diapers, contamination would have kept on seeping into the well."

"Exactly," agreed Rev. Whitehead. "But because you and Dr. Snow were able to convince the committee to act, no one could get water from the Broad Street pump after Constable Lewis got sick."

"He fought for his life for eleven days," reflected Dr. Snow.

"Eleven days during which the epidemic would have kept on raging if it hadn't been for you, Dr. Snow," put in Mrs. Weatherburn as she refilled his teacup.

The doctor smiled and raised his cup to me. "And you,

Eel. If you hadn't tracked down Mrs. Eley, I'm not sure the committee would have made the decision they did."

Nothing would bring Bernie and the others back. But we had made a difference. Removing the handle of the Broad Street pump had saved lives.

CHAPTER TWENTY-SIX
Henry and Me

There is only one more part of my story to tell.

One evening at Dr. Snow's house, I was surprised to find Dr. Farr from the General Register Office, where I had written out the list of deaths, and also Mr. Edward Huggins and a kind-looking woman he introduced as his wife.

It was quite a crowd for Dr. Snow, who didn't usually entertain. Especially since Rev. Whitehead was there as well. And so was Henry.

I had Mrs. Weatherburn to thank for Henry. As soon as she'd heard my whole story, she'd gotten a cab and the two of us had gone to fetch him from Mrs. Miggle. Then she had bought us clothes and sent us to school.

"And if that evil man you call Fisheye comes after you again, he shall find himself transported to Australia," she threatened. "After all, Dr. Snow has connections with the queen."

Still, I knew Dr. Snow couldn't take care of us. His work came first, and he was rarely home. We didn't know what might happen next. Until this night.

Dr. Farr spoke first. "Dr. Snow invited me here so I could help illuminate your past."

Henry leaned in close to me and said in a loud whisper, "What's he talking about? What's *illuminate*?"

Dr. Snow smiled. "Don't worry, Henry. All Dr. Farr means is that he is able to tell you something about your family."

Dr. Farr addressed me. "Young man, perhaps if you had not adopted that odd nickname of yours, I might have realized this sooner. But seeing your extraordinary eyes that day got me thinking.

"And since I work in an office that keeps records, I did some research. It was just as I thought. Now brace yourselves, lads," he told Henry and me. "I am here to tell you that your father worked for me when you were little. He had your eyes, Eel, the very same."

"You mean, sir, that our father helped to keep records?" I asked.

I remembered that day when I'd sat with the clerks in Somerset House, copying down that list for Dr. Snow.

Keeping records of those who had died might seem a trivial thing. But from all Dr. Snow had taught me, I knew such information could change things—it could save lives.

"After your father died, I lost track of you both," Dr. Farr was saying. "I'd heard your mother had fallen into distress and had remarried, badly. But when she passed away, all trace of you boys was lost."

Henry's mouth was open, and I realized mine was too. I wondered where Dr. Farr's story was headed.

"I thought I recognized you that day, but I couldn't be sure," Dr. Farr told me. "Your father had brought you in when you were quite small; I'm sure you wouldn't remember. You should know that he always spoke of both his sons with pride."

My father had worked in the General Register Office! He had helped keep the data that Dr. Snow depended on.

"So a mystery of your past is revealed," said Dr. Snow.

There was more.

"Now for your future," said Dr. Snow. He nodded at Mr. Edward Huggins, who spoke next.

"As I thought, Eel, I can't get you your situation back. But I can offer you something else. My wife and I lost our only baby to flu a few years ago." He reached out and took her hand.

"Eel and Henry, if you're willing, we'd like you to come live with us," Mr. Edward offered. "We promise to send you to school. Eel, you could even follow in Dr. Snow's footsteps and be a physician someday if you wanted."

If I became a doctor, I could do experiments and change things, just as Dr. Snow was doing with his theory. And I might earn enough so that maybe, someday, I could offer Florrie a chance to do art. I could imagine her drawing maps and charts and medical illustrations—all to help make people's lives healthier and better. Florrie would like that.

Around me, the adults applauded. Henry smiled shyly, burying his head in my side. I had only one question.

"Yes," said Mr. Edward. "Dilly is welcome too."

EPILOGUE

1855
Wednesday, September 26

At the invitation of Dr. Snow and Rev. Whitehead, Florrie, Henry, and I went to a committee meeting at St. James' Church.

The pump on Broad Street had been without its handle for more than a year, and the neighborhood had petitioned that it be put back. The well had been repaired so waste couldn't seep underground, and cholera had not appeared again in the neighborhood. So it was no surprise that the vote came out in favor of opening the pump again.

Afterward, we said warm goodbyes to Dr. Snow and Rev. Whitehead, who were off to drink tea and compare notes on the papers they had written about the spread of cholera. Florrie's employer, a reform-minded lady named Mrs. Mary Tealby, had been so impressed with Florrie's role in making Dr. Snow's map, she had given Florrie special permission to come. (It helped that Dr. Snow himself had paid the good lady a visit and asked for Florrie's help in illustrating the final version of his map.)

Florrie, Henry, and I began walking, catching up on our lives and reflecting on all that had changed in the past year. I led the way, and somehow found myself heading toward Blackfriars Bridge.

"We can't get home too late," said Henry, who loved living with Mr. Edward and his wife just as much as I did. For me it was being able to breathe again—a chance to use my mind for more than just scavenging.

On the bridge, I leaned over to look at the dark sweep of the Thames below us. I thought of my mudlarking days, trudging through the slimy mud, covered in filth from head to toe.

"Have you seen Thumbless Jake recently?" Florrie asked softly.

"No," I said, putting my hand on Dilly's head to keep her close. "Not for a long time."

But the words Jake had spoken that morning the Great Trouble began came back to me: "Ain't we all riverfinders? Put on this earth to try to get by, one day at a time. We're all we've got under this sky. We need to play fair and take care of one another."

We had done that as best we could: Dr. Snow, Rev. Whitehead, Florrie, and me.

Thumbless Jake. I wondered what would happen to

him. It would be nice to think he could find his way back to Hazel and his children, though somehow I didn't think so. He'd had such trouble in his life.

But then again, so had all of us that summer when the Great Trouble had come to Broad Street.

And somehow, we had survived.

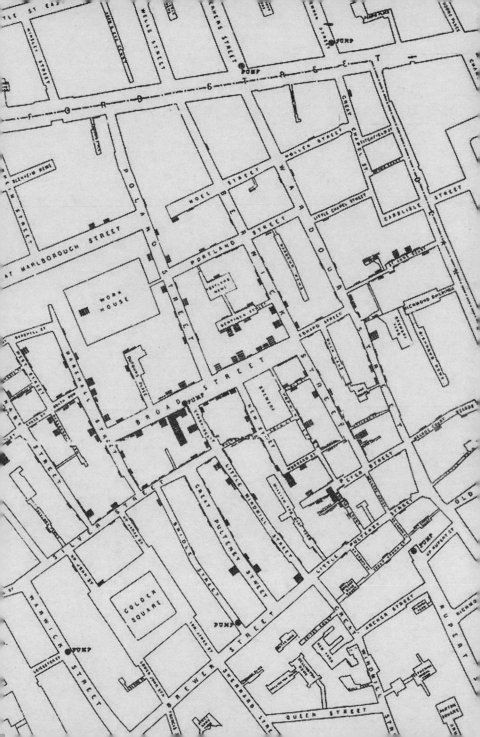

AUTHOR'S NOTE
A Reader's Guide to
THE GREAT TROUBLE

Many readers ask where I get my ideas. My inspiration often comes from what I read, and that's certainly true for *The Great Trouble*. Several years ago I came upon a book by Steven Johnson called *The Ghost Map: The Story of London's Most Terrifying Epidemic—and How It Changed Science, Cities, and the Modern World.*

Replica of the Broad Street pump outside the John Snow, a pub on what is now Broadwick Street, London
Photograph by Deborah Hopkinson

The Ghost Map tells the true story of Dr. John Snow and the Broad Street cholera epidemic of 1854. While *The*

Great Trouble is historical fiction, the story mirrors the progress of the epidemic during those late-summer days so long ago, when 616 residents died. Some of the action is compressed into fewer days (see the timeline for a summary of actual events), and I've given my fictional characters Eel and Florrie major roles in solving the mystery.

The real Dr. Snow created the now-famous map that revealed that deaths from cholera, sometimes called the blue death, were clustered around the Broad Street pump. By interviewing residents (including the sons of Susannah Eley, who died in her home several miles away after drinking the water), Dr. Snow was able to demonstrate a link between drinking from the Broad Street well and getting the disease.

Thanks to Dr. Snow's testimony at the committee meeting on September 7, the pump handle was removed on September 8. In his book, Steven Johnson calls that day "a turning point"—an important moment in the history of public health, when action was taken to protect citizens based on scientific theory.

The investigations didn't stop then. Later that fall, Dr. Snow and Rev. Henry Whitehead were asked to join the St. James Cholera Inquiry Committee to continue to study the epidemic. Rev. Whitehead, who had no medical training, disagreed with Dr. Snow's theory at first. But as he talked to families, he became convinced that Dr. Snow was right.

It was also Henry Whitehead who discovered that baby

Frances (Fanny) Lewis was the index case that started the epidemic. This led to an excavation of the cesspool at 40 Broad Street in the spring of 1855. In his report of May 1, the surveyor, Jehoshaphat York, noted that the bricks lining the cesspool were decayed. The Broad Street well was less than three feet away, and the surrounding soil was saturated with human waste. In other words, when Sarah Lewis emptied her baby's diapers into the cesspool, the cholera bacteria seeped through bricks and soil to contaminate the water in the well.

As in our story, after little Frances Lewis died on Saturday, September 2, the epidemic naturally waned because no new contamination of the well was taking place. But her father, Constable Thomas Lewis, fell ill on Friday, September 8, the very day the pump handle was removed. Had the well not been closed, the epidemic would undoubtedly have killed more people because Mrs. Lewis had begun emptying her husband's waste into the cesspool. When no new epidemics struck the neighborhood, the pump handle was eventually restored in September 1855.

Dr. John Snow is known today as a pioneer both in public health and in the field of anesthesiology. But until I read *The Ghost Map,* I hadn't heard of him. My journey to find out more took me to books, websites, museums, and libraries, including the Wellcome Library in London, which specializes in the history of medicine.

Finally, I found myself standing on Broadwick Street,

which used to be called Broad Street. There's a replica of the pump there, and a pink slab of granite nearby marks where it once stood. In 2011, as it must have been in 1854, the street was the center of a bustling neighborhood. I couldn't help reaching down to touch the stone as I imagined what it had been like to live then. And that is how this book came to be.

ABOUT THE CHARACTERS

The Great Trouble includes both fictional characters and historical figures. Eel, Henry, Florrie, Fisheye Bill Tyler, the Griggs family, Abel Cooper, Nasty Ned, and Thumbless Jake are fictional. Historical figures include Dr. John Snow, Rev. Henry Whitehead, William Farr, and Dr. Snow's housekeeper, Jane Weatherburn.

I have also used the names of some actual Soho residents. The brothers John and Edward Huggins really were the owners of the Lion Brewery, though I have no reason to think they were not both perfectly nice gentlemen. Their nephew Hugzie is fictional.

People who lived at 40 Broad Street included a tailor, "Mr. G.," who became the fictional Mr. Griggs. Constable Thomas Lewis and his wife, Sarah, also lived at that address, along with a son, an infant daughter named Frances, and a daughter named Annie, who in a later census was listed as an embroiderer. (Thus she became Annie Ribbons in my book.) Susannah Eley, who lived in Hampstead, was the widow of a munitions factory owner. Knowing of her fondness for water from the Broad Street well, her sons had a bottle delivered to her daily.

Additional information about major historical figures in the story is included in the following sections.

Dr. John Snow (1813-1858)

John Snow was born in York, the eldest of nine children. His father, William, began as an unskilled laborer and was eventually able to purchase a farm. John's parents wanted to give their children a primary education, so John went to school until the age of fourteen.

In 1827, he was apprenticed to William Hardcastle, a family friend who was a surgeon apothecary in Newcastle upon Tyne, a coal-mining town. It was there, in 1831, that John first became acquainted with cholera. He moved to London to continue his medical training in 1836 and set up his practice in the city two years later.

In 1846, the London dentist James Robinson became the first doctor in England to demonstrate ether. Gases like ether and chloroform were important because they allowed people to undergo surgical and dental procedures without pain. John Snow began doing his own research on anesthesia and often experimented on guinea pigs, mice, frogs, and other animal subjects. He also designed an inhaler and began assisting dentists and surgeons. He became so well known for his skill that he gave chloroform to Queen Victoria when she gave birth to Prince Leopold in 1853.

At the same time, Dr. Snow was researching cholera. By 1854, when the Broad Street epidemic occurred, he was studying the relationship between cholera outbreaks and London's water supply.

Even after the success of the Broad Street investigation in 1854, not everyone in the field of public health agreed with Dr. Snow's theory on cholera. It was not until 1866, partly thanks to Henry Whitehead, that Dr. Snow's conviction that cholera was a waterborne disease was fully accepted. Unfortunately, John Snow was not there to see that development. He suffered what was apparently a stroke and died on June 16, 1858. He was only forty-five. Today he is remembered for his pioneering research in anesthesia and epidemiology.

Rev. Henry Whitehead (1825-1896)

Henry Whitehead is an unlikely hero in the history of cholera. He had no medical or public health training. He was born in Ramsgate, where his father was the headmaster of a school. Whitehead attended the University of Oxford, receiving his degree in 1850.

His first assignment in London was as assistant curate at St. Luke's Church on Berwick Street. Just shy of thirty when the cholera epidemic broke out, he was a familiar and comforting figure to the families of the neighborhood.

Rev. Whitehead remained unconvinced by Dr. John Snow's theory until the two of them were thrown together on the St. James Cholera Inquiry Committee. In January 1855, after reading the monograph about the Broad Street epidemic that Dr. Snow had prepared and gathering information from the residents, Rev. Whitehead came to believe that Dr. Snow was right.

In 1865 and 1866, when cholera again broke out, Rev. Whitehead published articles reminding the public of Dr. Snow's earlier work. In 1874, when he left London for a position in Brampton, a farewell dinner was held in his honor. During his speech, he called his old friend "as great a benefactor in my opinion to the human race as has appeared in the present century."

Dr. William Farr
(1807-1883)

William Farr was born into a large family in the village of Shropshire. It was his good fortune to attract the attention of a local benefactor, Joseph Pryce, who paid for his education. When Pryce died in 1828, he left William money, which the young man used to pursue medical training. William became interested in medical statistics, urging that physicians record the exact reason for a person's death. In 1838, he joined the General Register Office for England and Wales, where he was responsible for the collection of medical statistics. He stayed with the office until his retirement in 1880.

Dr. Farr came late to believing that contaminated water, not miasma, caused the spread of cholera. It was not until the cholera epidemic of 1866, eight years after Dr. John

Snow's death, that he fully supported Dr. Snow's theory. Today Dr. Farr is remembered for developing a national vital statistics system, which provided data to public health officials and served as an example to other countries.

THE SETTING

The Great Trouble takes place in Victorian London. Queen Victoria ruled Great Britain from 1837 until her death in 1901; to date, hers is the longest reign of any British monarch and the longest of any female monarch in history. This period has become known as the Victorian era.

In the summer of 1854, when our story opens, London was a rapidly growing city of two million. Scavengers were the recyclers of Eel's London: night-soil men emptied cesspools; mudlarks and other riverfinders recycled wood, coal, and other things from the Thames. There were ragpickers and bone collectors. Pure-finders collected dog waste and sold it to tanners, who used it in making leather goods.

But the scavengers could not keep up. London was a city without a sewer system capable of dealing with its animal and human waste. Much of it ended up in the Thames, especially as indoor toilets, which led to the river, became more prevalent.

London would have to wait until the Great Stink of 1858, a summer when the stench became so bad that laws were finally passed to authorize the construction of a modern sewer system. It took sixteen years and 318 million bricks to build eighty-three miles of sewers, guided by the vision of the chief metropolitan engineer, Joseph Bazalgette. But that is another story!

CHOLERA—YESTERDAY AND TODAY

Cholera is caused by the bacterium *Vibrio cholerae*. Although Robert Koch is usually credited with being the first to see the bacillus under a microscope in 1883, an Italian researcher named Filippo Pacini identified it in 1854, the same year as the Broad Street epidemic. In 1965, the name *Vibrio cholerae Pacini 1854* was adopted in honor of Pacini's earlier, largely forgotten discovery.

As Dr. Snow theorized, cholera is spread primarily through contaminated water. According to the website of International Medical Corps:

> Cholera is an acute diarrheal disease caused by an infection in the intestines that can kill even a healthy adult in a matter of hours. Symptoms, including severe watery diarrhea, can surface in as little as two hours or up to five days after infection, and can then trigger extreme dehydration and kidney failure. With such a short incubation period, cholera can easily explode into an outbreak. . . . Cholera is caused by ingestion of the bacterium, *Vibrio cholerae*. The infection is spread through contaminated fecal matter, which can be

consumed through tainted food and water sources or because of poor sanitation and hygiene, like unwashed hands. (International Medical Corps. "Basic Facts on Cholera." *http://internationalmedicalcorps.org/page.aspx?pid=475*)

It was Dr. Snow's fervent hope that "the time will arrive when great outbreaks of cholera will be things of the past." While this is true in many parts of the world, there are still tens of thousands of deaths from cholera every year. According to a 2012 fact sheet on cholera from the World Health Organization, there are an estimated three million to five million cases and 100,000 to 120,000 deaths every year.

Cholera struck in Haiti following the devastating earthquake of January 12, 2010. The disease had not been seen in Haiti in more than fifty years, but the conditions following the earthquake resulted in water contamination. As of 2012, there were more than a half-million cases of cholera, and seven thousand deaths from it since the earthquake.

The primary treatment for cholera today is relatively simple: reversing dehydration with an oral rehydration solution. Sometimes patients require IV fluids. Some residents of the Golden Square were able to survive the blue death by drinking lots of clean water.

EPIDEMIOLOGY AND PUBLIC HEALTH

Dr. John Snow is often called the father of epidemiology, the study of how and why diseases spread. The United States Department of Labor describes the work of these scientists this way: "Epidemiologists investigate the causes of disease and other public health problems to prevent them from spreading or from happening again. They report their findings to public policy officials and to the general public." (http://www.bls.gov/ooh/life-physical-and-social-science /epidemiologists.htm#tab-2)

DR. JOHN SNOW'S WORDS

I have invented most of the dialogue for both the fictional and the historical figures in *The Great Trouble*. But I could not resist including Dr. John Snow's own words, as quoted by Henry Whitehead:

"'You and I,' he would say to me, 'may not live to see the day, and my name may be forgotten when it comes, but the time will arrive when great outbreaks of cholera will be things of the past; and it is the knowledge of the way in which the disease is propagated which will cause them to disappear.'"

TIMELINE OF
THE BROAD STREET
CHOLERA EPIDEMIC

1854

MONDAY, AUGUST 28: Five-month-old Frances (Fanny) Lewis, daughter of Sarah and Thomas Lewis of 40 Broad Street, falls ill with diarrhea and vomiting.

THURSDAY, AUGUST 31: "Mr. G.," a tailor who also lives at 40 Broad Street, along with nineteen or twenty other people, falls ill. Twenty-nine-year-old Henry Whitehead, assistant curate at St. Luke's Church, is called out to several homes where people have been struck.

FRIDAY, SEPTEMBER 1: Mr. G. dies of cholera. A yellow flag is placed on Berwick Street as a warning, and carts begin removing bodies.

SATURDAY, SEPTEMBER 2: Baby Frances Lewis dies on Broad Street. Several miles away in Hampstead, Susannah Eley, a fifty-nine-year-old widow who has been drinking Broad Street water delivered by her sons, dies after a sixteen-hour illness. At Middlesex Hospital, the nurse Florence Nightingale begins seeing patients brought in every half hour from Broad Street and elsewhere in the Soho district.

SUNDAY, SEPTEMBER 3: Dr. John Snow, who lives a half mile away on Sackville Street, hears about the cholera epidemic. He goes to inspect the popular Broad Street pump and takes water samples for inspection.

MONDAY, SEPTEMBER 4: Mrs. G., the widow of the tailor, falls ill with cholera. Dr. Snow returns to Broad Street and begins asking questions of the residents.

TUESDAY, SEPTEMBER 5: Mrs. G. dies in the morning. Dr. Snow goes to the General Register Office in Somerset House to ask William Farr for records of recent deaths.

THURSDAY, SEPTEMBER 7: Dr. Snow appears before an emergency committee of the board of governors of St. James Parish and convinces them to remove the handle of the Broad Street pump.

FRIDAY, SEPTEMBER 8: The pump handle is removed. Thomas Lewis, father of Frances Lewis, develops symptoms of cholera.

TUESDAY, SEPTEMBER 19: Thomas Lewis dies.

THURSDAY, NOVEMBER 23: St. James Parish forms an inquiry committee to look further into the cholera epidemic, which killed 616 people. Dr. Snow and Rev. Whitehead are invited to join.

MONDAY, NOVEMBER 27: An inspection of the Broad Street well is conducted, but no holes are found.

MONDAY, DECEMBER 4: Dr. Snow presents his cholera map at a meeting of the Epidemiological Society of London.

TUESDAY, DECEMBER 19: The *Gazzetta Medica Italiana* contains an article by researcher Filippo Pacini, who reports microscopic findings from postmortem exams of cholera patients. His research will not become widely known until after his death.

1855

SATURDAY, JANUARY 27: The London publisher J. Churchill releases an expanded version of *On the Mode of Communication of Cholera,* a monograph by Dr. John Snow. Dr. Snow gives a copy to Rev. Whitehead, who is continuing to conduct interviews with Broad Street residents for his own report.

TUESDAY, MARCH 27: While investigating death records in the General Register Office, Rev. Whitehead is drawn to the following entry: "At 40, Broad Street, 2nd September, a daughter, aged five months, exhaustion, after an attack of Diarrhoea four days previous to death." Rev.

Whitehead finds that Mrs. Lewis emptied diapers into the cesspool, and he suspects this may be the index case and the cause of the well's contamination.

MONDAY, APRIL 23: A surveyor, Jehoshaphat York, excavates the cesspool at 40 Broad Street and the surrounding area.

TUESDAY, MAY 1: York presents his report, showing that sewage was backing up in a drain and the cesspool's bricks were decaying. Sewage from the cesspool had been seeping into the Broad Street well, less than three feet away.

WEDNESDAY, JULY 25: The St. James Cholera Inquiry Committee completes its work, which includes reports from York, Dr. Snow, and Rev. Whitehead. The committee concludes that the cholera outbreak "was in some manner attributable to the use of the impure water of the well in Broad Street."

WEDNESDAY, SEPTEMBER 26: Based on a petition from residents, a decision is made to reopen the Broad Street pump.

READ MORE!

This bibliography includes websites and books I used in researching my story. While some are for adults, I believe young readers who want to learn more would enjoy Steven Johnson's *The Ghost Map,* as well as the books listed in the final section.

WEBSITES

DR. JOHN SNOW
The Department of Epidemiology at the UCLA Fielding School of Public Health maintains a website devoted to Dr. John Snow: www.ph.ucla.edu/epi/snow.html.

JOHN SNOW'S MAP
To view a large version of Dr. Snow's map, you can go to the following link on the UCLA website: www.ph.ucla.edu /epi/snow/highressnowmap.html.

CHOLERA
To learn more about cholera, see internationalmedical corps.org.

EPIDEMIOLOGY
To learn more about epidemiology, visit www.ph.ucla.edu/epi.
To find out about epidemiology as a career, look at the United States Department of Labor's Occupational Outlook Handbook: www.bls.gov/ooh/life-physical-and -social-science/epidemiologists.htm.

BOOKS ABOUT DR. JOHN SNOW, CHOLERA, AND LONDON

Hempel, Sandra. *The Medical Detective: John Snow, Cholera and the Mystery of the Broad Street Pump*. London: Granta Books, 2006.

Johnson, Steven. *The Ghost Map: The Story of London's Most Terrifying Epidemic—and How It Changed Science, Cities, and the Modern World*. New York: Riverhead Books, 2006.

Mayhew, Henry. *London Labour and the London Poor: A Selection by Rosemary O'Day and David Englander*. Ware, Hertfordshire, England: Wordsworth Editions, 2008.

Mitchell, Sally. *Daily Life in Victorian England,* 2nd ed. Westport, CT: Greenwood Press, 2009.

Morris, Robert D. *The Blue Death: Disease, Disaster, and the Water We Drink*. New York: HarperCollins, 2007.

Picard, Liza. *Victorian London: The Tale of a City, 1840–1870*. New York: St. Martin's Griffin, 2007.

Vinten-Johansen, Peter, Howard Brody, Nigel Paneth, Stephen Rachman, and Michael Rip. *Cholera, Chloroform, and the Science of Medicine: A Life of John Snow*. Oxford: Oxford University Press, 2003.

BOOKS FOR YOUNG READERS ABOUT EPIDEMICS

Anderson, Laurie Halse. *Fever, 1793*. New York: Simon & Schuster, 2000.

Barnard, Bryn. *Outbreak: Plagues That Changed History.* New York: Crown, 2005.

Farrell, Jeanette. *Invisible Enemies: Stories of Infectious Diseases.* 2nd ed. New York: Farrar, Straus and Giroux, 2005.

Lowry, Lois. *Like the Willow Tree: The Diary of Lydia Amelia Pierce.* New York: Scholastic, 2011.

Murphy, Jim. *An American Plague: The True and Terrifying Story of the Yellow Fever Epidemic of 1793.* New York: Clarion Books, 2003.

ACKNOWLEDGMENTS

The Great Trouble is a book about community and friendship, and I could not have written it without the help and support of many colleagues and friends. My editor, Allison Wortche, made me feel that bringing this story to life was possible, and I am grateful for all her hard work—her careful and thoughtful comments helped to shift this story in important ways. Thanks to Jenny Golub for her incredible copyediting expertise, which helped to make the manuscript better. Thanks to Jinna Shin for a wonderful design and Stephanie Dalton Cowan for her fabulous cover. I owe a longtime debt of gratitude to the entire team at Knopf and Random House, with special thanks to Nancy Hinkel, Adrienne Waintraub and her fantastic team, and Anne Schwartz and Lee Wade. Steven Malk, my agent, reminds me always to write from my heart. Thanks also to the staff at the Wellcome Library in London and to members of the John Snow Society, who keep Dr. Snow's work and memory alive.

I am fortunate to be part of a professional community

at Pacific Northwest College of Art that encourages and values creativity. I am grateful to our board and our president, Tom Manley, and to my colleagues—especially the advancement team of Deanna Bredthauer, Deniz Conger, Jacquie Gregor, Killeen Hanson, Juliette Simmons, Melinda Stoops, Alisha Sullivan, and Luann Whorton—for their support.

I am profoundly grateful to my friends and family. My dear friend Michele Hill, to whom this book is dedicated, always encouraged me to write and was there when my first story was published. I miss her. Debbie Wiles reminds me every day that telling stories is important and inspires me to keep going. Thanks to Vicki Hemphill, Ellie Thomas, Teresa Vast, Michael Kieran, Sheridan Mosher, Kristin Hill, Bill Carrick, Cyndi Howard, Elisa Johnston, Maya Abels, Kathy Park, Greg and Becky Smith, Michele Kophs, and Nancy Barrows. I hope that my sisters, Bonnie Johnson and Janice Fairbrother, enjoy Dilly (modeled after our beloved Kona, whom we lost this year). Like me, they are dog lovers (perhaps we're making up for a canine-deprived past). And finally, to my husband, Andy, and children, Rebekah and Dimitri—you give me joy every day and I love you.

ABOUT THE AUTHOR

Deborah Hopkinson is the acclaimed author of many books for young readers, including *A Boy Called Dickens,* a Kids' Indie Next List Selection; *Annie and Helen,* a Junior Library Guild Selection; *Sky Boys: How They Built the Empire State Building,* an ALA-ALSC Notable Children's Book and a *Boston Globe–Horn Book* Honor Book; and *Sweet Clara and the Freedom Quilt,* winner of the IRA Children's Book Award. She is also the author of *Into the Firestorm,* a novel for young readers about the 1906 San Francisco earthquake and fire.

Deborah Hopkinson lives with her family in Oregon. Please visit her online at DeborahHopkinson.com.

READ AN EXCERPT FROM

INTO THE FIRESTORM:
A Novel of San Francisco, 1906

BY DEBORAH HOPKINSON

ROAD KID

"Hey, kid. Get back here and empty your pockets."

Nicholas Dray whirled to see a burly policeman pointing a black club right at him. He froze in astonishment. This should not be happening. Not to Nick the Invisible.

Nick could count only three things he was good at. First, he could pick cotton. Working cotton—planting, thinning, chopping the weeds away with a hoe, and picking—was about all he'd done for most of his eleven years.

Nick wasn't bad at writing, either. Oh, not putting words together to tell a story or anything, just making letters and words look nice. Back in Texas, he would often come home after working in the fields and sink down with his back against their wooden shack. Before long he'd be scratching in the dust with a stick until Pa yelled at him to finish his chores or Gran called him in to eat some steaming-hot corn bread.

Being invisible was Nick's third and newest skill. He'd only gotten good at it since becoming a road kid, since that morning a few weeks ago when he'd finally taken off from the Lincoln Poor Farm for Indigents and Orphans.

Nick had worried a lot about whether he'd be able to make it to California from Texas. But between begging rides from farmers and even hopping a few freight trains, things had gone pretty well. Not one policeman or official-looking person had paid him any mind. In fact, Nick had gotten so confident, he'd begun to think of himself as Nick the Invisible.

So how could he have let this policeman sneak up on him? How could it be that now, when he'd finally arrived in San Francisco, just where he wanted to be, he wasn't invisible at all?

"Hey, kid, didn't you hear me the first time? Get back here and empty your pockets." The policeman's yell drowned out the clanking of a cable car. The big man lumbered closer, looking like a giant bear, with bushy red eyebrows sprouting every which way. "I saw you stick your grimy hand into that vegetable cart."

"You can't send me back. I didn't take anything, Bushy Brows," Nick mumbled out loud, pushing off into a run.

And that was true enough. Nick hadn't stolen a thing—at least not yet. He'd only stopped to feast his eyes on the bright lettuces and cabbages and breathe in the fresh, sweet scent of oranges piled in neat rows. He couldn't help it. He was that hungry.

Nick pulled his old brown cap over his curly hair and lunged into the crowd. His wild hair could be a problem. It made him easy to spot—and made it easy for policemen like Bushy Brows to remember him.

Nick never used to mind his hair. For one thing, Gran kept it cut close during cotton season so as to keep his head cooler. She'd always told Nick his hair was a gift from his mother. Since his mother had died when he was born, Nick didn't carry any real memories of her, not the kind that make you sad, anyway. There was just that faded wedding photograph in a cracked frame that Gran kept free of dust as best she could.

"My, how Janet would've laughed to see such a shock of wild curls wasted on a boy," Gran would say in her soft drawl as Nick sat on an upturned bucket while she trimmed away. She always made sure to scatter the cut locks to the wind so the birds would have something for their nests.

Nick risked a glance back at the policeman. Another mistake. He wheeled forward again to find a well-dressed man with a thick brown mustache barreling down on him.

At that moment, Bushy Brows let loose an ear-splitting cry. "Stop. Thief!"

"A thief, eh? I'll teach you, young ruffian," growled the man, thrusting out a long black umbrella.

Crack!

"Ow!" Nick cried out as the umbrella hit his shins. The man made a grab for him, but Nick twisted away, his heart pounding. His head felt light from not eating.

Nick did his best, though. He skipped around businessmen in suits and hats, ladies in long dark skirts and crisp white shirtwaist blouses, deliverymen toting crates and boxes. Veering onto the cobblestone street to avoid bumping a tottering elderly lady, he found himself face to face with a snorting horse pulling a cart.

"Easy, Betsy," the driver crooned to his mare. "You watch it, boy. Lucky for you I ain't driving one of those fast new automobiles."

By now Nick was panting. He could feel drops of sweat trickle down the back of his neck. This should have been easy, but everything was going wrong. And then, just when he felt sure he'd left the police officer behind, he tripped.

Nick threw out his hands, scraping his palms hard on the sidewalk. He groaned and closed his eyes, feeling a wave of sickness wash over him. It all sounded far away: laughter and voices, the ironclad wheels of wagons clattering along on cobbled streets, cable cars screeching and clanging.

"I got you." Nick felt something hard jab into his back.

The large, round officer loomed above him, panting slightly. Nick looked up and tried to bring the man into focus. His eyebrows were enormous, with hairs sticking out in all directions like a thicket of blackberry branches.

The officer poked. "Get up, boy."

Nick got to his feet slowly. He staggered a little, feeling dizzy with hunger. "I didn't take anything, sir. Honest."

"You talk funny. You're not from here, are you? We got enough problems with the Chinese without snotty runaways roaming the city," the policeman grumbled. "Now turn out your pockets and tell me where you live."

Nick's heart sank. He stuck his hands into his pockets, closing his right hand tightly around the two coins he'd kept safe for so long.

What was it Mr. Hank had said that last day? "Once a picker, always a picker."

A cotton picker. Maybe, after all, the boss man had been right. Maybe that's all he'd ever be.

COTTON PICKER

Before. Before the Lincoln Poor Farm for Indigents and Orphans, there'd been Mr. Hank's farm. Nick and Gran had landed there in late summer, after they'd been driven off their sharecrop.

"I ain't happy about taking in an old lady and a kid," Mr. Hank had grumbled. "But I'm short of hands right about now. If you can keep up and put in a full day's work, you can stay."

"My grandson picks cotton faster than a grown man, Mr. Hank," Gran assured him. "I wouldn't be surprised if he picks a hundred pounds a day when the cotton is at its peak."

Mr. Hank scoffed, "He looks too skinny. Probably lazy, too." And from that moment, Nick made up his mind to try.

For the next two weeks, Nick picked from daybreak to dusk. He came close to bringing in a hundred pounds in a single day, but he never could quite make it.

"Grandson, I'll give you two bits tonight if you can do it," Gran said on that last morning. He bent to give her a sip of tepid water from the dipper.

"We don't have a dime to spare, Gran, never mind a quarter." Nick's heart turned over, but he had to grin. "Not yet, anyhow. But before long, I'll make enough to get us out of here."

"It would sure be nice to have our own house again," she murmured, shaking her head. "I never thought I'd miss that shack on Mr. Greene's place. But where do we go now? No farmer wants to give an old lady and a skinny kid a sharecrop."

"I've got that all worked out, Gran. We're gonna leave Texas and head to California," Nick said all in a rush. He'd been thinking about this plan for so long but had never put it into words before. "I got the idea even before Pa left and we lost the sharecrop. You remember Miss Reedy, my teacher? She told us all about the city of San Francisco. That's where we'll go."

"California? That sounds as far away as the moon." Gran's voice was hoarse, but there was still a twinkle in her warm brown eyes.

"We can get there, Gran, I know it." Nick held her

hand in his. He could feel how work had weathered and hardened her skin. "Miss Reedy said San Francisco was the Paris of the Pacific. You know, like Paris, France. It's a great, golden place on a bay of blue water. Tall buildings reach as high as the clouds, and cable cars run up and down hills as steep as cliffs."

Gran shook her head a little. "Now what would we do in a grand place like that?"

"I'll get a job," Nick went on, talking fast, half afraid she'd start laughing and call it a foolish dream. And maybe it was, but now that he'd started, he couldn't stop. "We'll find us a little room. Miss Reedy says there's sometimes a cool fog in San Francisco, so it won't be hot and dusty like here. And we'll never pick cotton again."

"Never pick cotton again . . . ," Gran repeated in a whisper. She looked into Nick's eyes. "Why, I believe I can just see you on the streets of that bright city."

Gran's breath seemed ragged and uneven, as though it hurt to talk. She pressed his hand, then let go. "Now you get on, or Mr. Hank will be mad. And don't fret about me—Elsie Turner promised she'll look in later."

The fields that day had been thick with pickers. Men and women, some as old as Gran. And children, too. Others were so small they could only toddle behind their mamas. Nick knew most everyone by name. Elsie Turner's daughter, Rebecca, had taken to tagging after him.

"Daddy says I can't stop till I fill my bag or I'll get a whipping," she'd whined just the day before. "You pick sooo fast, Nick. Can't you *pleeease* give me some of yours?"

Rebecca asked him this just about every day. As usual, Nick growled in return. "Go away, Rebecca. You can't pick if you're jabbering the whole time."

But that hadn't stopped her questions. "You ever been to school, Nick?"

"Not much," he admitted. "We used to live on a sharecrop before we came here. I'd go to school sometimes, when my pa didn't need me in the fields. I liked parts of it just fine."

"I'm five, too little for school," announced Rebecca. "Did you pick cotton when you were five?"

Nick grunted. "I've picked cotton since I could walk."

On that last morning, Rebecca hadn't bothered him at all. Nick found himself looking around for her. He spotted her in the next row over, her shoulders slumped. Rebecca moved slowly, her small bag trailing behind her. Nick thought a breeze might knock her over.

There had been dew in the early dawn. Nick didn't like picking on dewy mornings. For one thing, it made his clothes damp and cool just when the morning was chill. Worse was what the dampness did to skin.

Nick's fingers were so callused and rough from

picking, he didn't suffer much. But he figured the morning dew had made little Rebecca's skin soft. So soft the hard points of the cotton bolls had dug into her fingers, drawing tiny pricks of blood each time she reached inside to pluck out the white fiber.

"Rebecca," called Nick in a loud hiss. "Scurry up to me and hold open your bag."

In a flash, Nick pulled out an armful of cotton and stuffed it into her sack. Rebecca went back to her row, her bag dragging behind her, too miserable to smile her thanks.

By mid-afternoon, an enormous sun filled a glaring white sky. Nick's sack could have been packed with river rocks, it was that heavy. He wanted to rest, to stretch out between the rows of cotton and fall asleep on the warm earth. Nick felt everything was against him—the sun, the heat, the prickly cotton bolls, the stubborn cotton itself.

I can't give up, Nick told himself. Even if the bag got so heavy it made him weave like a drunken man. Even if the muscles in his shoulders burned into his bones. Sweat stung his eyes, but Nick didn't stop to wipe it away. He made himself keep picking, steady and quick.

Now grab the cotton at its very roots. Now pick it out clean. Right hand, left hand, both together.

A hundred pounds, a hundred pounds, he chanted silently. *A hundred pounds for Gran.*

TOMMY

"You're one of those road kids, ain't you?" The thick-browed policeman kept hold of one of Nick's sleeves and poked at him with his club as if he were checking the tenderness of a piece of meat.

Nick opened his mouth. Nothing came out. He was caught. And then Gran's words came back to him. *I believe I can just see you on the streets of that bright city.*

Nick bent to snatch his cap off the ground. Then he squirmed—hard—wrenching his sleeve out of the policeman's grip.

"Why, you . . ."

Nick willed himself to *move,* feet flying, dodging and ducking through the crowd. He could hear Bushy Brows pounding behind him, panting and wheezing. He sounded madder than a wasp, and he sure didn't seem ready to give up.

"Stop that boy!"

Up ahead, Nick saw two men unloading a large crate from a wagon. They were blocking the sidewalk and seemed to be having trouble getting the crate through a doorway. Nick could hear the men arguing. A small circle had gathered to watch and give advice.

"Turn the crate the other way."

"Put it down first and measure the opening."

The workers backed away from the doorway, calculating their next move. Nick grabbed his chance. Slipping into the circle, he darted between the men and the doorway. He crawled through the legs of the bystanders. And he came out the other side.

Bushy Brows wouldn't catch him now.

Nick slowed to a trot, his breath coming in short gasps. He should duck in somewhere and hide. He couldn't be sure Bushy Brows would give up the chase.

Nick hurried along, head down, not meeting people's eyes. And so at first he didn't notice he'd entered a different neighborhood. It was full of small, busy shops, with bright wooden signs and barrels of food crowding the sidewalks. Even the air had changed, and his nose caught the scent of smoke, fish, and spices.

The streets now were filled mostly with men in simple blue cotton clothes. He walked behind a man who wore a small round hat. His hair was pulled into a long dark braid that hung down his back.

Chinatown. He was in Chinatown. Since he'd arrived in San Francisco a few days ago, Nick had heard people on the street talk about Chinatown, but this was the first time he'd come here.

Nick ducked into a doorway. Next to him, bins displayed fruits and vegetables. Above his head was a large sign with flowing, inky black symbols on it. That, he figured, must be Chinese writing. Nick felt a thrill of excitement. He'd come to the city from Texas. But these people had traveled from the other side of the world.

The world really is big, just like Miss Reedy was always telling us, Nick thought.

The writing reminded Nick of Miss Reedy's penmanship lessons—his favorite part of school. Mostly Nick and everyone else in the run-down one-room schoolhouse did lessons in chalk or pencil. Once a week, though, Miss Reedy brought in several real Waterman pens for them to try, along with her prize possession, an old-fashioned glass inkwell decorated with flowing silver leaves. She placed it on the center of her desk, almost like a vase of flowers on a table.

If he closed his eyes, Nick could still see the glass sparkle as that inkwell caught the rays of the morning sun streaming in the window. He'd sure never seen anything like it at home—or anywhere else, for that matter. It was just an ordinary object, a container for ink. But he couldn't help wondering where it had come from. Someone, far away, must have worked hard to make it so beautiful.

All at once the door behind him opened. A Chinese man emerged and nodded. Without thinking, Nick slipped inside. Bushy Brows wouldn't think of looking for him here.

Nick took a few steps and stopped uncertainly. It seemed safe—no one was in sight. He tiptoed behind a shelf toward the back of the store. Maybe he could hide here a little while and then slip out the back into the alley.

Suddenly Nick heard a noise. Sprinting quickly across the wooden floor, he entered a small storeroom in the back. He crouched behind some barrels full of peanuts and held his breath. He didn't think he'd been spotted.

Nick heard voices—a customer must have come in. But Nick couldn't understand a word of the language that was spoken.

Maybe I should run for it, Nick thought. On the other hand, what was the chance of Bushy Brows finding him? Better to stay put.